Also by Jo Nesbø

JO NESBØ

ILLUSTRATED BY
Mike Lowery

ALADDIN NEW YORK LONDON TORONTO SYDNEY NEW DELHI

DOCTOR PROCTOR'S FART POWDER

SILENT (BUT DEADLY) NIGHT

ALADDIN

An imprint of Simon & Schuster Children's Publishing Division

1230 Avenue of the Americas, New York, NY 10020

First Aladdin hardcover edition October 2017

Copyright © 2016 Jo Nesbø

English translation copyright © 2017 by Tara Chace

Originally published in Norway in 2016 as *Kan Doktor Proktor redde jula?* by H. Aschehoug & Co.

Published by arrangement with Salomonsson Agency

Illustration copyright © 2017 by Mike Lowery

For information about special discounts for bulk purchases, please contact Simon & Schuster Special Sales at 1-866-506-1949 or business@simonandschuster.com.

The Simon & Schuster Speakers Bureau can bring authors to your live event. For more information or to book an event contact the Simon & Schuster Speakers Bureau at 1-866-248-3049 or visit our website at www.simonspeakers.com.

Designed by Karin Paprocki

The text of this book was set in Perpetua Regular.

Manufactured in the United States of America 0917 FFG

2 4 6 8 10 9 7 5 3 1

Library of Congress Cataloging-in-Publication Data

Names: Nesbø, Jo, 1960- author. | Lowery, Mike, 1980- illustrator.

Title: Silent (but deadly) night / Jo Nesbø ; illustrated by Mike Lowery.

Description: First Aladdin hardcover edition. | New York : Aladdin, 2017. |

Series: Doctor Proctor's fart powder ; 5 | Summary: Dr. Proctor, Nilly, and Lisa set out to find Santa and save Christmas after the king of Norway sells the rights to the holiday to money-hungry Mr. Thrane.

Identifiers: LCCN 2017007139 (print) | LCCN 2017025643 (eBook) |

ISBN 9781534410015 (eBook) | ISBN 9781534409996 (hc)

Subjects: | CYAC: Christmas—Fiction. | Santa Claus—Fiction. | Inventors—Fiction. |

Adventure and adventurers—Fiction. | Flatulence—Fiction. | Norway—Fiction. | Humorous stories. |

BISAC: JUVENILE FICTION / Humorous Stories. | JUVENILE FICTION / Action & Adventure / General. |

JUVENILE FICTION / Holidays & Celebrations / Christmas & Advent.

Classification: LCC PZ7.N43825 (eBook) | LCC PZ7.N43825 Sil 2017 (print) | DDC [Fic]—dc23

LC record available at https://lccn.loc.gov/2017007139

SILENT
(BUT DEADLY)
NIGHT

Five Days before Christmas Eve

THIS IS A STORY that starts at dusk on the last Sunday in Advent.

Snow lay thick over Norway, especially over Oslo, especially, especially over Cannon Avenue, and especially, especially, *especially* over the peculiar, crooked blue house at the very end of the street, where pretty soon someone was going to have to suck it up and shovel the front walkway, past the snow-laden pear tree and all the way out to the gate. Didn't anybody live there? Oh yes, someone did. There were footsteps, both small and large, from the gate to the front steps. There were candles burning inside the frozen windowpanes, and smoke was rising from the chimney.

And in the kitchen a neighbor girl named Lisa was sitting at the table staring dreamily into space while she listened to Juliette, the cheerful woman stirring a pot on the stove and telling a romantic Christmas story about two lovers who were together, lost each other, and then found each other again on Christmas Eve.

"I loooove romantic stories that are sad in the middle," Lisa sighed rapturously. "Especially if they're a little spooky, too."

Juliette Margarine laughed and poured more

milk into the casserole pan. "That, *mademoiselle* Lisa, is because you're sitting in a warm, cozy house and aren't out there"—she gestured toward the window—"with those creepy, nasty invisible beings who sneak around before Christmas."

Just then the door hinges in the front hallway squeaked and a cold gust of wind blew into the kitchen. They looked at each other. Someone—or something—had just entered the house. They heard footsteps creaking on the wood floor in the hallway.

"Wh-wh-who's there?" Juliette asked, her voice trembling. No answer.

"Who . . . ?" Juliette began, but put her hand over her mouth in fright.

Something terrifying had appeared in the hallway door: a stack of firewood, a stack of cut, split birch logs hovering about eight inches off the ground.

"Oh no, a pile of hovering firewood!" whimpered Juliette. "What do you want with us? We're only two innocent, defenseless women."

"Eat!" the stack of firewood said.

"*Mon Dieu!*" Juliette said, because she's French and *mon Dieu* is French for "my God"! "Are you going to eat us both, or will eating the smaller one be enough? Are you going to eat the whole house or eat . . . ?"

"Eat rice porridge!" the firewood said.

"Oh, then come sit over here by the woodstove," Juliette said, and went back to stirring the pot.

The stack of wood floated over to the crackling woodstove and tumbled into the firewood basket with a clatter. From behind the woodpile that had seemed like it was floating, an unusually small boy came into view. He had an even smaller upturned nose and the tiniest freckles you've ever seen. He brushed the snow off his sweater and picked a few birch chips out of his bright red hair and teeny-tiny ears.

"Hungry, Nilly?" Lisa asked.

"Am I hungry?" the minuscule boy asked, and then wiped his nose on his sweater sleeve. "Let me explain. . . ."

"Oh no," Lisa mumbled.

"When I set out on that polar expedition, I put my own life on the line with one goal in mind." He raised an unbelievably short index finger. "To save women and children . . . well, mostly women . . . from cold and hunger. With rudimentary tools, no means of communication or navigational instruments, and completely alone, I wrestled my way through that inferno of snow, which threated to inundate me multiple times. But I did not give up, because I'm Nilly, and Nilly never gives up. Nilly—"

"Nilly, you just went to the garage for more firewood," Lisa said, pointing out the kitchen window to where the moon shone on the rickety wooden structure over by the gate.

"Exactly!" the boy said. "And now the emaciated, famished Nilly is a teensy bit disappointed that those selfsame women and children—mostly women—that he risked his young life for haven't made it just the *slightest* bit further along in preparing the"— Nilly played dead, rolling his eyes and then slumping to the floor—"rice porridge."

"Nilly, you were gone for only *five* minutes."

"And it's going to be another only five minutes until it's ready," Juliette said with a smile. "Especially if you'll get up and set the table, Nilly."

Nilly popped up, leaped up onto the kitchen counter, opened the cupboard, and got out some bowls.

Just then there was a bang from beneath the floor-boards. "What was that?" Lisa cried.

"Oh, probably just Victor inventing something."

They heard shuffling footsteps coming up the stairs from the basement, and a moment later an unusually tall, skinny man entered the kitchen. He had big, bushy hair, a wispy beard, and a beaming smile and wore a blue inventor's lab coat and a pair of sunglasses that upon closer inspection turned out to be swim goggles.

"Sweetheart! Friends!" he declared, and gave Juliette a loud kiss on the cheek. "Eureka!"

"That means 'I have found it,'" Lisa whispered to Nilly, who had crawled up next to her on the wooden bench at the table.

"Nilly is *aware* of that, silly friend," Nilly said. "What did you invent, Doctor Proctor?"

"I will tell you, my friends. I have improved Raspa's time soap so that you no longer need a special time-traveling bathtub to travel through time and space." He held up a small shampoo bottle containing a small amount of raspberry-red liquid. "You pour the soap into any old bathtub, bucket, or pool and stir until bubbles form. Then you just dive down, think of somewhere far away and a date sometime in the past, and when you stand up, then—tada!—there you are!"

"*Mon amour*, you're a genius!" Juliette said, and gave Professor Proctor such an enthusiastic hug that he turned a little red in the face.

"You'll probably get a medal from the National Endowment of the Farts for this one!" said Nilly, who was now standing on the bench. "You can sell time soap to the whole world. You'll be rich!"

"Unfortunately, probably not," Doctor Proctor said with a smile. "Turns out these are the last few drops of Raspa's time soap remaining, and now that Raspa's gone, no one has the formula for how to make more."

"But what we *can* make more of is rice porridge!" said Juliette, and set the casserole pan in the middle of the table. "Have at it. Let's see if we can finish all this!"

With that they lunged for Juliette's rice porridge. Because there's only one thing Lisa and Nilly like better than Juliette's rice porridge, and that's Doctor Proctor's Jell-O. Unfortunately, Nilly had yet to find a way to make other foods that he liked less well taste like rice porridge or Jell-O. Fortunately, he had come up with a workaround. Nilly happened to love anything that tasted like caramel, so he always kept a bottle of caramel sauce in his pocket. His mother wasn't exactly a master chef, so when he and his sister ate dinner, Nilly had learned to distract their mother (for example by yelling, "Look! A seven-legged spider!") and then super quickly giving his food a little squirt of caramel sauce. Even though it must be said that fish sticks with caramel sauce taste a little weird, and pea soup with caramel sauce even weirder.

Luckily, now they were in Juliette and Doctor Proctor's kitchen. And while they slurped and gulped and *mmmm*ed, Juliette Margarine told them a story about how her wealthy family back in France used to celebrate Christmas in a big, cold castle, with duck for dinner and gifts before bed on Christmas Eve. They always had plenty of servants, but no friends or relatives.

"With my family it was the opposite," Doctor Proctor said, getting up to turn on the radio. "My parents had a teeny-weenie, warm little house with no servants, but tons of relatives on Christmas Eve. There were so many of us the house was practically bursting. We oozed out the windows and doors."

He found the radio station that was playing requests, where contacts, coworkers, classmates, colleagues, cousins, and companions could dedicate songs to each other and include a brief Christmas greeting.

"We were all inventors," Doctor Proctor continued, "and everyone would talk over each other, describing their latest inventions. For Christmas Eve dinner we would eat something new that my mother and grandmother had invented and then give each other Christmas presents we'd invented ourselves."

"Like what?" Nilly asked in between mouthfuls.

"Oh, maybe muscle gloves that let you shovel tons of snow without getting tired or skis that made it impossible for you to fall down. But usually just things that exploded in fun ways. And then there was that year Aunt Inga invented a box of candy where all the pieces talked when you opened the box. They were all babbling over each other about how delicious they were, right up until they all finally started squeaking in unison: 'Pick me! Pick me!'"

"Ho, ho, ho!" Nilly chuckled. "And did you guys have Santa Claus?"

Doctor Proctor stared into space for a minute before answering. "I suppose we did the typical Norwegian thing. After dinner on Christmas Eve my dad would go out. He always said he had to help Santa. And then a while later Santa would stop by with some presents. Then he would say he had a lot of people to visit and disappear as quickly as he'd come."

"That is *exactly* what happens at our house!" Lisa said. "Only I can tell from Santa's shoes that he's really just my dad, dressed up."

"What about you, Victor?" Juliette asked. "Could you tell if Santa was actually your father, just dressed up? Did your dad come back again right after Santa left?"

"No," Doctor Proctor said, sounding distant and staring vacantly out the window. "My dad never came home until *really* late. I mean, I think helping Santa was a big and important job for him."

"Ha-ha-ha," Nilly said sarcastically.

"Well, your Christmas Eve definitely sounds like more fun than at my house," Lisa said. "In my family we always give each other sensible presents—new backpacks for school and money to participate in band and things like that. My dad makes sure we do all the traditional Norwegian stuff. We join hands and walk around the Christmas tree, *always* in the correct direction. And when we open our presents, my mom collects the wrapping paper and ribbons so we can use them again the following year. And she saves all the cards and writes estimates on them of what she thinks the presents cost so the following year we can give them a present that costs about the same amount."

"You have a very thorough mother," Doctor Proctor said.

Lisa laughed. "Last year," she said, "I got a little present wrapped in regular writing paper, which was actually used. I mean, there was writing on it. The card just said 'from Santa.' It was a snow globe—you know, one of those glass balls that you shake and then it snows inside."

"Yes, of course. I know about those," Doctor Proctor said. "In fact, my great-great-grandfather invented them."

"Anyway," Lisa continued, "my mom was really annoyed that it just said 'from Santa' because now she has no idea who we have to give an equivalent present to this year! And I didn't want to tell her that obviously we only know one person who would think to wrap a present that way!"

Juliette and Lisa looked over at the little redheaded fellow, who didn't seem to be paying any attention. Instead he was playing air trumpet while whistling the trumpet solo in "Silent Night" on the radio.

"Did he *say* it was from him?" Doctor Proctor asked, glancing at Nilly. Lisa shook her head.

"Well, then you can't rule out that it might actually have come from Santa," Doctor Proctor said, scratching his beard thoughtfully.

"Um, hello?" Lisa groaned. "Santa, really?"

"You don't believe in Santa Claus?" Doctor Proctor asked in surprise.

"Uh, no! Do you?"

"Noooooo," Doctor Proctor said, dragging it out. "I don't *believe* in Santa Claus. I actually *know*—"

Juliette loudly cleared her throat. "What do you know?" Lisa asked.

"I . . . uh, know . . . ," Doctor Proctor said, and then glanced over at Juliette, who gave him a cautionary look.

"Let me put it this way," Doctor Proctor said. "I *know* that in recent years fewer and fewer people believe in Santa because he's getting lost in all the present buying we do. People nowadays believe more in the Christmas sales at Mr. Thrane's department store than they do in Santa Claus. Every Christmas that goes by, Mr. Thrane gets richer and richer, while Santa, poor guy . . . Well, no one needs him and his simple little gifts anymore."

"You just made it sound like Santa Claus exists," Lisa said with a laugh.

"I—" Doctor Proctor began, but Juliette cut him short with a determined throat clearing.

"What does *your* family usually do for Christmas?" Juliette asked Nilly in order to change the subject.

Nilly made a few strangely smothered, gurgling

sounds before he managed to swallow enough rice porridge to be able to speak.

"It always depended on whether or not my mom was dating anyone. If she was, my sister and I would go spend it with my grandfather, when he was alive. And he would read to us."

"The Christmas story, you mean?" Juliette asked.

"No," Nilly said, helping himself to more porridge. *"Animals You Wish Didn't Exist."*

"Hmm, sounds festive."

"Super festive," Nilly said, shoveling food into his mouth. "For example, do you know why people in New York City started building skyscrapers with stores on the first couple floors and then residential space farther up?"

The others just looked at him.

"Vampire giraffes," Nilly said.

"Nooo," Juliette said, and leaned farther over the table. "Do tell!"

"There's not much to tell," Nilly said. "Just that vampire giraffes have these really ghastly fangs that they bite with, and then they suck blood and beer like this. . . ." He loudly slurped rice porridge from his spoon.

"Yuck!" Lisa said.

"But, luckily, they only come out at night," Nilly said. "Then they stagger around the dark city streets on their long, skinny giraffe legs. They're so tall and their legs are so skinny that the cars just drive right underneath them and most of the motorists don't even notice them. And the vampire giraffe doesn't care about cars; of course it's just looking for beer and blood. Which is why it's so great that it has such a long giraffe neck. Well, great for it, really, not great for us, because with those legs and that neck, it can reach the fourth floor, at least. So if you like to sleep with your window open"—Nilly waved his spoon around, causing a little porridge shower—"then you'd better not have your bedroom or your refrigerator lower than the fifth floor."

"Mon Dieu!" Juliette whispered as Doctor Proctor chuckled beside her.

"But people in Australia's Northern Territory have it even worse," Nilly said, his eyes wide. "The scariest, most remote place on this earth . . ."

"Nilly!" Lisa cried.

Juliette raised one eyebrow and looked at her. "He's just making this stuff up!" Lisa groaned.

"So what?" Juliette said. "Continue, *mon ami.*"

"Flying dogs," Nilly said, stretching his arms out to both sides. "Huuuuuge doggies with bat wings. At dusk they come flying out of their caves in clouds so big they darken the entire sky. A hundred years ago they started encroaching on more densely populated areas, and according to my grandfather, it became the worst infestation since tsetse elephants ravaged the African continent."

Juliette put her hand over her mouth in horror and then said, "*Mais non!* And these flying dogs sucked blood from humans?"

"Blood?" Nilly asked, cocking his head. "Why in the world would they do that? We're talking about *dogs*. They pooed!"

"Uh . . . *pooed?*" Juliette asked, turning to Doctor Proctor. "What is that in French, Victor?"

"I'll explain later, my dear."

"It just tumbled down," Nilly said, putting his hands on his head. "People got it in their hair, on their hats, on their bald heads, in their yards, on the roofs, patios, and swimming pools. And these were no little dogs on leashes with owners that have those little plastic bags to clean up after them. The poop was several feet deep in some places, runny brown muck that people slipped on, waded through, and sometimes drowned in. Oh, and the smell! Hey, does anyone else want more rice porridge?"

"No, thank you," the other three all answered simultaneously, watching as Nilly scooped the rest of the runny, white muck into his bowl.

"So they put a bounty on the flying dogs," Nilly said. "There were quite simply too many of them. I mean, the Australians are really fond of their backyard barbecues. So right around sunset they'd fire up their grills, shoot straight up into the air and— *thump!*—a fresh dog-steak would land smack on the grill. They liked to eat them with bread and mustard and ketchup, and according to my grandfather, that's actually where the term 'hot dog' came from. Now, speaking of ketchup . . ." Nilly pulled the bottle of caramel sauce out of his pocket and looked at the porridge in his bowl.

"Totally unnecessary," Lisa said, shaking her head.

"Agreed," Nilly said, and stuffed the bottle of caramel sauce back in his pocket. "Anyway, my grandfather went to Australia to write about the flying dogs in *AYWDE*."

"AYWDE?" Juliette asked.

"Animals You Wish Didn't Exist," Lisa and Doctor Proctor responded in unison.

"And then one night when my grandfather was at a barbecue at someone's house, something *else* tumbled onto the grill," Nilly said. "They had shot down some kind of flying billy goat, antlers and all!"

Lisa slapped her hand to her forehead. "Nilly, you're lying!"

"Am not!" Nilly said.

"Are too!" Lisa put her hands on her hips. "Can you go home, get your grandfather's book, and show me the flying goat, then?"

"Of course not."

"Ha! You see? Because you're *lying!*"

"Now, now, kids," Doctor Proctor said, but Nilly had already leaped onto the table.

"It's not in the book because a goat with meat that tender is not an animal you wish didn't exist," Nilly declared, standing on the table. "Quite the contrary, it's an animal you're glad exists because you can't imagine a more mouthwatering Sunday roast."

"Well put, Nilly," Doctor Proctor said. "So well put that, as a reward, you have permission to do the dishes."

"The dishes . . . ? Reward?"

"Yes, and you're certainly welcome to ask your best friend if she wants to help you dry."

Nilly moaned and closed his eyes. His red-haired head and his short arms drooped. Then he raised his head again, opened one eye, and looked at Lisa.

"Heeeeey, Liiiiisa . . . ?"

"Fine!" she said, pulling the napkin off her lap in annoyance. "I'll help you." She started gathering up the dishes.

"Oh, Lisa, you're so nice!" Nilly jumped down beside her and flung his arms around his best friend.

"Yes, and you always manage to take advantage of that!" she said, and gave him a little swat on the head, although not that hard, and it's possible she might have been smiling a bit, too. Because if Lisa was to be honest—and she almost always was—there were actually a couple of things she loved even more than Jell-O, and one of them was Nilly.

Nilly and Lisa did the dishes while Juliette and Doctor Proctor drank coffee at the kitchen table and hummed along to the Christmas music on the radio's call-in show. Lisa told them that what she wanted for Christmas was a kinder world where things were a little better for poor children. She didn't see Nilly, who was standing behind her making faces and yawning as loudly as he could. And Nilly explained that he wanted a little time soap so he could go back to the Moulin Rouge in

Paris in 1922 and watch the dancers dancing the cancan onstage.

"I looove cancan dancers," Nilly said with his eyes closed, so he didn't see Lisa, who was making faces and rabbit ears behind his back. And then all four of them suddenly froze because the voice on the radio had just said Doctor Proctor's name.

". . . Victor Proctor would like to dedicate this song to his girlfriend, Juliette Margarine, and wishes everyone on Cannon Avenue, including Lisa and Nilly, a very merry Christmas!"

And then an accordion started playing and a woman began singing in French. "Édith Piaf!" Juliette said with a smile.

"What's she singing about?" Lisa asked.

"Something romantic that's a little sad in the middle," Juliette said. "But listen. Now it gets cheerful!"

And then Doctor Proctor danced with Juliette, and Lisa asked if Nilly wanted to dance too, and he said sure, but only if they danced the cancan. So Lisa and Nilly stood next to each other, put their hands on their hips, and kicked their legs into the air as high as they could while yelling, "Cancan!"

"THIS IS AN EXTRA NEWS BULLETIN! THIS JUST IN! TODAY THE KING SOLD CHRISTMAS TO MR. THRANE!"

The voice on the radio had spoken so abruptly and what it said was so shocking that Doctor Proctor and

Juliette slipped in the middle of a pirouette and Nilly and Lisa tipped over backward, each with one foot up in the air.

"MR. THRANE ANNOUNCED THAT FROM THIS POINT FORWARD CHRISTMAS COULD ONLY BE CELEBRATED BY PEOPLE WHO HAD PURCHASED AT LEAST TEN THOUSAND CROWNS' WORTH OF PRESENTS FROM ONE OF THRANE'S DEPARTMENT STORES."

Still Five Days to Go until Christmas Eve

LISA AND NILLY ran out of the blue house at the end of Cannon Avenue and out the gate. A group of children was caroling in front of one of the other houses. They were singing "Joy to the World" with Mr. Madsen conducting them, the way they did every Christmas. In another yard a man was up on a ladder decorating his apple tree with tinsel, blinking lights, and a tall hat on top.

"Hi, Nilly and Lisa," said a little girl in a Santa hat who was sitting on a sled in the middle of the street and looking up at them. "When Santa comin'?"

"In one hundred and two hours," Nilly said. "All you have to do is start counting."

"One, two, twee, fouw . . ."

Lisa and Nilly stopped in front of the gates to numbers 14 Cannon Avenue and 15 Cannon Avenue.

"Do you think it's true, Nilly, that there might not be a Christmas this year?"

"Nonsense," Nilly said. "Just look around. Everything around here is just the way it is every single Christmas, right?"

"But—but . . ."

"We're going to go home to bed now, Lisa. And when we wake up in the morning, then we'll see that all this was just a dream."

"A *terrible* dream."

"Worse than a monster-chasing-you-while-you-try-to-run-through-a-swamp nightmare."

"Do you promise?" she asked.

"Trust me, Lisa. I've dreamed of worse things than what we're dreaming right now. And tonight I'm going to play you 'O Come, All Ye Faithful.'"

"Okay."

Then they each ran into their houses, Lisa into the red one and Nilly into the yellow one.

"ISN'T IT SHOCKING?" said Lisa's mother, who was sitting in her chair knitting when Lisa walked into the living room.

"Just awful," grumbled the commandant, whose recliner was tilted so far back he was practically lying down. He turned up the volume as the TV reporter looked directly into the camera and said:

"SO MR. THRANE'S COMPANY OWNS

THE RIGHTS TO EVERYTHING CHRISTMAS-RELATED. IN OTHER WORDS, FROM NOW ON NO ONE CAN CELEBRATE CHRISTMAS WITHOUT AUTHORIZATION FROM MR. THRANE. THE FOLLOWING THINGS ARE ALL STRICTLY FORBIDDEN: CHRISTMAS CAROLS, CHRISTMAS COOKIES, BOUGHS OF HOLLY, CHRISTMAS DINNERS, CHRISTMAS CHURCH SERVICES, OR EVEN SAYING 'MERRY CHRIST-MAS' WITHOUT MR. THRANE'S APPROVAL. MR. THRANE SAID IN HIS PRESS RELEASE THAT PERMISSION WILL BE GRANTED *ONLY* TO REGISTERED MEMBERS OF CHRIST-MAS. AND THE ONLY WAY TO QUALIFY FOR MEMBERSHIP IS TO SPEND AT LEAST TEN THOUSAND CROWNS ON CHRISTMAS PRES-ENTS FROM ANY OF THRANE'S DEPARTMENT STORES BEFORE CHRISTMAS EVE. THIS IS ACCORDING TO MR. THRANE HIMSELF AT

THE PRESS CONFERENCE HE GAVE EARLIER THIS EVENING. . . ."

"Ugh, ugh, and ugh!" Lisa's mother said as the greasy face of Mr. Thrane, their former Cannon Avenue neighbor, filled the screen. Below his wet, smacking lips there was a stack of wobbling chins. Then his mouth opened and started talking:

"I, MR. THRANE, WARN THOSE WHO PLAN ANY ATTEMPT TO CIRCUMVENT THESE RULES THAT WE HERE AT MY CORPORATION, THRANE INC., HAVE HIRED OUR OWN CHRISTMAS POLICE TO ENFORCE THE RULES, AND THEY ARE ON PATROL AS OF NOW!"

Mr. Thrane thrust his face and mouth so close to the camera that it fogged up as he whispered:

"SO, YOU OUT THERE—YOU DESPICABLE CHEAPSKATES WHO HAVEN'T SPENT TEN THOUSAND CROWNS ON GIFTS YET AND

ARE BURNING SEASONAL CANDLES OR DRINKING EGGNOG RIGHT NOW—BLOW THEM OUT! POUR IT OUT!"

Then Thrane took two steps backward so that almost all of his massive body fit in the shot. He lit up in a smile and tugged on his suspender straps.

"BUT, MY DEAR CHRISTMAS MEMBERS, TO YOU I WISH A MERRY CHRISTMAS. YOU, WHO HAVE DONE WHAT GOOD CONSUMERS SHOULD, WHO HAVE SPENT TEN THOUSAND HAPPY CROWNS SUPPORTING SOCIETY AND THE BUSINESS COMMUNITY BY BUYING THINGS YOU MAY NOT NEED. THAT IS WHAT MAKES THE WHEELS GO ROUND. SO, TO ALL OUR VALUED CHRISTMAS MEMBERS, LET'S ENJOY THIS PEACEFUL CHRISTMAS SEASON TOGETHER. AMEN!"

The commandant clicked the TV remote and Mr. Thrane disappeared.

In the ensuing silence they heard the voices of the carolers out on the street. They were singing "Silent Night." But the song ceased abruptly when a scared, breathless woman's voice shouted, "Stop this! Stop this right away! You're not allowed to use the word 'Christmas'! Go home all of you. Go home!"

"They can't do that, can they?" Lisa said. "They can't just ban people from celebrating Christmas. I mean, it's the best holiday we have, and it belongs to everyone."

"I must admit that's what I thought too," the commandant said. "Until now at any rate."

"So what will Christmas be like now?" Lisa asked.

"We'll have to wait and see, Lisa my dear," the commandant said, and then sighed.

Lisa heard the distant sound of music and walked over to the living room window.

The music seemed to be coming from one of the huge, well-lit houses up in the snow-covered hills above Cannon Avenue. They were playing "White Christmas." They must have been having a big party up there. Maybe the music was actually coming from the Thrane family's house. They had moved to one of those houses up there the year before. Everyone on Cannon Avenue had been happy to see the boastful Thrane and his bullying twin sons, Truls and Trym, move off their street. But the three Thranes still sometimes came back to visit, strutting up and down Cannon Avenue as if stopping by to see their former neighbors, but everyone knew that Mr. Thrane was only there to show off how rich and powerful he'd become.

"So, are you still commandant of that outdated old fortress?" Mr. Thrane had asked Lisa's father the last time he'd strolled down Cannon Avenue, and sort of jokingly thumped him on the back. "Have you guys even shot anything with your cannons in the last three hundred years, hmm?"

And Lisa's dad had tried to smile pleasantly, but

Lisa had noticed that he hadn't quite pulled it off. And afterward, as Mr. Thrane had continued swaggering down Cannon Avenue, Trym and Tuls had seen their opportunity to yell "Flatu-Lisa!" and "Are you still hanging out with that speckled dwarf?"

Up in the hills the music was turned up a little louder still.

"I can see that you're worried, Lisa," said her mother, who had come over to stand beside her by the window. "Sure, ten thousand crowns is a little more than we were planning to spend, but we'll buy what we need to. We promise. We'll qualify for Christmas membership, and you'll get to celebrate. So don't fret about it, Lisa."

"That's not what I'm thinking about, Mom."

"It—it isn't?"

"Mom! I'm thinking about all the other people out there who can't afford it, who won't get to celebrate Christmas this year at all."

"Oh, right," her mother said. "Yes, of course. That is a shame for . . . uh, a lot of folks. But, unfortunately, there's not much we can do about that."

"But it must be possible for us to do a *little* something about it, right?"

Her mother stroked Lisa's cheek. "You've always been a brave, stubborn girl when you feel you're in the right, Lisa. But now that you're getting bigger, I'm sure you'll see that there are some things that just can't be changed. And you have to live with them."

"Sure, Mom—"

"Have you already had dinner?"

"Yes, but is it fair for Christmas to—"

"And have you done your homework?"

"Yes, but—"

"Then it's bedtime, Lisa. Tomorrow is a school day, you know. And maybe after we've slept on it we'll find that all this business about Christmas isn't so bad."

"Mom, think about—"

"No more thinking today, Lisa. Good night, sweetie."

Lisa sighed. "Dad?"

"Yes, honey?" the commandant growled.

"Do you think we're dreaming right now, that maybe this isn't really happening? That when we wake up tomorrow there'll be Christmas after all?"

The commandant swiveled his chair to look at her. "I think that's a wonderful thought. Hold on to it, honey."

AFTER LISA WENT upstairs to her room, her mother sat back down with her knitting. "Lisa sure is concerned about the world, about the environment, poverty, peace, and all that," she said.

"Hmm," the commandant said as he browsed through the newspaper. "You mean that fully automatic machine gun I bought her for Christmas might not be quite the right gift, hmm?"

Lisa's mother dropped her knitting in her lap.

"Arnold! You didn't! Please tell me you did not buy her a fully automat—" She stopped when she realized that he'd lowered his newspaper and was watching her.

"Huh," she said. "You were joking?"

He nodded slowly and confirmed, "Joking."

"Well, in that case, *ha-ha*."

"Do you want me to read you the weather forecast now, dear?"

"Yes, please, but on the subject of Christmas presents, dear: Maybe you should ask for something more expensive than a tie for Christmas this year."

"Hmm, you mean so we'll spend more than ten thousand crowns? In that case I wish I had a new missile-that-never-misses for the fortress, since we only have one, and it would be nice to have a second."

"I see. So how much does a missile like that cost?"

"A million crowns."

"Arnold! We don't have a . . . Wait! Were you joking?"

"Joking."

"In that case, ha-ha-ha. Go ahead and read the weather forecast now, dear."

NILLY UNLOCKED THE door of the yellow house, walked inside, and listened. The radio, stereo, and TV were all off, so his sister must be out, as usual. He snuck up the stairs and heard moaning from behind the closed bathroom door. He tiptoed toward his bedroom and thought he'd made it there undetected when he heard his mother's voice yap from the bathroom, "Nilly? Where have you been?"

"At Doctor Proctor's place."

"You and Lisa spend too much time there. I *don't* like it!"

"Would you rather I be here, then?"

"No. Good heavens, no! But be somewhere else. With all the crazy things that Proctor guy invents, that whole place is going explode someday, you mark my words."

"Mom, *this* whole place is going to explode if you don't manage to unleash the hounds in there."

"Hey, constipation is no laughing matter! How many times do I have to tell you that? Listen . . ." A deep gut gurgle could be heard from behind the bathroom door. "On a different subject, though, I need some cash. Ten thousand crowns, to be precise."

"Mom, I told you that kind of Christmas celebration isn't really important to me. I mostly cared about it when Grandpa was alive."

"For you, sure! You only think about yourself. What about a hardworking single mother? Shouldn't she get to celebrate Christmas? *I* want a Christmas, and I'm going buy myself a few little odds and ends for ten thousand crowns. Because *I'm worth it!* Do you hear me?"

"I heard what you said about hardworking, yeah. And, I mean, I don't doubt you're working hard right now, sitting in there, but how are you going to get ten thousand crowns if you don't want to work, Mom?"

"Want? Of course I *want* to! But I can't! I'm . . . weak. Is that somehow my fault? That's what I tell my doctor anyway. If I could quit being weak, then he wouldn't have to keep writing me doctor's notes to explain all my absences."

Nilly could hear her crying a little in there.

"Do you want me to make you some tea, Mom?"

"No, you nitwit! I want you to help me get ten thousand crowns! What about your bike?"

"You sold it when you and Roy or Ove or whatever his name was wanted to go on vacation to Majorca last year."

"Do I hear whining? Hey, we all need to do our part around here! We'll scrimp and save. You know, I don't even have toilet paper in here, just magazines."

"Maybe you ought to give up the magazines instead. Those are more expensive than toilet paper, you know?"

"Are you crazy? How else would we keep up to date on world affairs? What about your trumpet? That thing just makes a racket around here. It would be nice to be rid of it."

"The mouthpiece is ruined, and a new one costs a thousand crowns."

"Well, then, you don't need the trumpet, do you?"

"Mom, you can't sell a trumpet without a mouthpiece!"

His mother emerged from the bathroom, struggling to do up her pants.

"No, I guess not, but what about that pocket watch you got from your grandfather? Or that book of his?

Wouldn't those have some kind of value to collectors?"

"The pocket watch runs fast, and you're not touching *AYWDE!*" Nilly stared at his mother's distended gut. "Are you pregnant?"

"Ugh!" his mother snapped, and then slapped Nilly on the back of the head. Then she stopped, put her finger to her chin, and looked as if she were actually considering the possibility. But then she slapped his head again and flung open the door to his room. "Where's that book? Bring it here!"

"Never!" Nilly said, darting into the room ahead of her.

He propped his hands against her knees and managed to push her out, but when he went to shut the door, her arms were still inside and her fingers were feeling their way along his wall until they reached the spine of the thick, leather-bound book on the shelf over his bed. Nilly grabbed the monster swatter he kept lying next to his bed. He had gotten it from Doctor Proctor, who had said it was an invention that chased nightmares and general spookiness out of a bedroom after dark, but actually it just looked like a completely normal flyswatter. He slapped his mother's fingers with it.

"Ow! Ow!" Her fingers vanished, and he heard footsteps and his mother's voice moving away down the hall. "All right, all right. I'll ask Åke if he can

loan me some money, then. He owes me that much after that disastrous ferry ride to Denmark. Pregnant? Right, can you imagine?"

Nilly pulled the book off his shelf, flipped through it a little, kissed the picture of the tsetse elephant, and hid the book under the loose floorboard beneath his bed. Then he had the thought that his mother wasn't usually *so* awful. It was just the constipation that had her in such a bad mood.

Nilly took his trumpet off the nail on the wall, opened his window, and waved to Lisa across the street.

A few seconds later her bedroom window opened. Nilly took a breath and raised his trumpet to his lips. And then he started playing. Since the trumpet didn't have a mouthpiece, it didn't make much noise. Well, actually none at all, just a little dry air. But it had been that way for a long time. That's why he told Lisa every evening what he would be playing so she could close her eyes and imagine him playing that specific song. And right now he was playing "O Come, All Ye Faithful" so silently that only two people in the whole world could hear it, him and his best friend, Lisa.

LISA FELL ASLEEP singing "O Come, All Ye Faithful" in her head. And then she dreamed the most wonderful and strangest dreams. When she woke up, it had only just begun to get light outside, and her first thought was that all that business about Christmas had just been one of her strange dreams.

"Oh, how lucky!" she said, hopping out of bed and running downstairs.

Her father was sitting at the breakfast table holding a big newspaper in such a way that Lisa could see the entire front page. She stiffened as she read the headline that said in coal-black, all-capital letters: MR. THRANE BUYS CHRISTMAS.

Four Days Left until... You Guessed It: Christmas Eve

MRS. STROBE PEERED at the class over the top of her glasses, which were balanced on the tip of her long, pointy nose.

"Unfortunately, I have some bad news," she said. "As you know, we were going to have a class Christmas party the day after tomorrow, but it's been canceled because the school can't afford to spend ten thousand crowns to buy"—she snorted disdainfully and slapped her ruler hard against her desk—"things! Yes, Lisa?"

"Does that mean people who can't afford to spend that much money won't get to celebrate Christmas at all? They won't even be able to *whisper* 'Merry Christmas' to each other?"

"I'm afraid that's right, Lisa." Mrs. Strobe pushed her glasses back up her nose again. "Those of you who already know that you can't afford to celebrate Christmas, could you raise your hands?"

Lisa looked around. She counted one, two, three, four, five, six . . . and then Nilly. She looked back at the teacher's desk again—and saw that Mrs. Strobe was raising her hand too.

"Yes, yes," Mrs. Strobe said with a sigh. "I suppose we'll have to hope no one buys summer vacation next."

"What happens if we celebrate Christmas anyway?"

a timid, tear-filled voice asked from the row along the window. That was Birte. Birte wore eyeglasses that had a white bandage stuck on one of the lenses. No one really knew why. She'd always had it there, and Lisa sometimes thought that Birte, her parents, and everyone else had gotten so used to it that they'd just forgotten all about it.

"Then the Christmas police will come!" Cecilie said, from the row along the wall. "That's what my dad says. And they'll put you in jail, and you'll have to live on bread and water the whole Christmas season."

"Yup," said Konrad in the front row. "And they won't even release you for New Year's Eve. Plus, they don't have any windows in jail, so you won't even get to see the fireworks. You'll only be able to hear the bangs and how much fun everyone's having out there."

When the recess bell rang, Lisa and Nilly walked out into the schoolyard together. They stood over by what Nilly called the White Pyramid, which was the enormous pile of snow the janitor's snowplow had created in the middle of the schoolyard. During recess the schoolyard usually echoed with shouts and laughter, especially lately, when children were practicing building snowmen for the big snowman competition in the park surrounding the royal palace on "Little Christmas Eve," the day before Christmas Eve. But today it was oddly quiet. Children spoke to one another in whispers or stood by themselves stiffly or with their heads drooping. A single voice was heard from the top of the stairs to the gym. It was Birte.

"It's not fair!" she wailed in her timid, tear-filled voice. "Christmas should be for everyone! It's not fair. It's so not fair!"

A snowball whistled through the air and hit Birte's face with a wet *smack*. Everyone stared as Birte started waving her hands in front of her. The snowball had hit the other eyeglass lens, the one without the tape. So now they both looked like they had tape on them.

"Nilly, don't laugh!" Lisa whispered, and pinched his side.

"Ouch!" he said. "I'm not the one laughing. You are!"

And to her horror, Lisa realized Nilly was right, but she couldn't help herself. Birte looked so funny standing there. But then Birte's mouth contorted and she started sobbing. And Lisa felt it so deeply in her heart that she started crying too.

"I'm a terrible person," she said, and ran over to Birte to help her.

"No, here come the terrible ones," Nilly said under his breath.

And there they came, Truls and Trym, waddling through the schoolyard, each packing a snowball. Nilly could only determine that they had gotten even bigger over the last several months. Their jackets were open so everyone could see their T-shirts bulging out over their belts and in between their suspenders. In all caps, the T-shirts said MEMBER OF CHRISTMAS with Thrane Inc.'s three official Christmas rings—in red, yellow, and blue—underneath.

"Any more poor people here who want to steal from Thrane Inc. and our father?" they yelled.

No one responded.

"Didn't think so," Truls said.

"Me either," Trym said. "Didn't think so."

"Anyone who is a member of Christmas is invited to join us for eggnog tonight," Truls said. "Who's in?"

No one in the schoolyard moved.

"Who's in?" bellowed Trym, raising his snowball. Several hands zipped into the air.

"Merry Christmas!" Truls said, and with that the Thrane twins waddled back toward the A Building.

Nilly stood there watching Lisa, who had helped Birte brush the snow off her eyeglasses and clothes and put her arm around Birte's shoulder. And he watched the other kids, who just stood there, open-mouthed, watching the twins walk away. Then he climbed the White Pyramid. He struggled his way to the top of the loose snow heap. Once there, he turned to the others and cleared his throat.

"Dear friends!" His voice echoed in the schoolyard.

"Friends?" he heard someone whisper. "Doesn't he only have one friend?"

"These are cold, hard times!" Nilly proclaimed.

"It's called *winter*, you gnome!" someone yelled.

"At times like these we need to stick together. We can't let them intimidate us. Thrane Inc. took Christmas from us! I urge you to fight the Thranes and any other robbers or slobberers who try to clobber you!"

"That dwarf thinks he's going to save the world again," someone said with a dismissive laugh.

Then someone started singing: "Nilly, Nilly

bragger boaster! Let's toast his butt in a chestnut roaster!"

Nilly sighed.

"Would you listen to yourselves?" Nilly said. "You're only accepting this because you're scared of Truls and Trym and the Christmas police and Thrane Inc. and . . . grfff."

Nilly tried to keep talking, but nothing came out. His mouth appeared to be full of snow. And Truls was standing behind him holding him while Trym held another clump of snow, ready to jam it into Nilly's mouth.

"What was that you wanted to say about us and our dad, hmm?"

"Grfff," Nilly said.

"*More?* Is that what you said?" Trym asked. He turned the lump of snow around so Nilly could see the yellow stripe where the janitor's dog had peed.

"Grfff!!" Nilly screamed, his eyes wide, struggling to free himself.

"He definitely said *more*," Truls said, tightening his hold on Nilly.

And with that, Trym stuffed the yellow-striped snow into Nilly's small, and yet big, mouth.

"How does it taste, you pathetic lout?" Truls whispered into his ear.

"Rye horage wif ubba," Nilly replied.

"Huh?"

"Rye horage wif ubba!"

"Can you understand what the gnome is saying?" Trym asked.

"You're going to have to take the snow out," Truls said.

"There's dog piss on it," Trym said.

"Take the snow out, I said!"

Trym made a face and did what his twin brother

told him. Nilly gasped for air and then coughed.

"Say what you said!" Truls ordered.

"I said it tastes like rice porridge with butter!" Nilly yelled.

"Put the snow back in," Truls demanded.

And with that Trym filled Nilly's mouth back up and all they heard from him was more "grfff."

"That's what happens to anyone who resists!" Truls yelled at the rest of the kids, who had all gathered around the pile of snow called the White (and maybe a bit yellow) Pyramid.

"So buy or die!"

"Buy or die!" Trym yelled, raising a snow shovel into the air. "Buy or die!"

"Exactly!" Truls said. "And remember: Those who die must be buried!"

"Exactly!" cried Trym. He jabbed the shovel into the snow and lickety-split he had dug a deep hole in the White Pyramid. Truls picked Nilly up and stuffed "the little freak of a boy" into the hole.

"There," Truls said. "From snow you came and to snow you shall return, you freckled pygmy!"

Trym covered the hole over with snow, and soon Nilly was gone. When the hole was totally filled in again, Trym patted down the snow with the shovel.

"Anyone else who doesn't want to buy a bunch of stuff for Christmas?" Truls asked.

He received no response, because the bell rang right then.

In only a few seconds the schoolyard was emptied of kids. Apart from Lisa, who crawled onto the snow pile and started digging.

She dug and dug as fast as she could and finally she felt something hard. A head? But it wasn't moving! She took off her mittens so she could feel what she was doing as she scraped away the snow. Yes, some familiar bright red hair came into view. She kept scooping away snow until she was looking down into the opening where Nilly was sitting. He sat with his legs crossed and his chin resting on his hand as he stared thoughtfully ahead.

"Wha-what are you doing?" Lisa asked, breathing hard.

"I'm thinking," Nilly said without looking up.

"You're . . . *thinking*?"

"Yes, my dear Lisa. I'm thinking that we have to do something. Think of all the poor little kids who have been looking forward to receiving Christmas presents all year long, the ones whose parents don't have ten thousand crowns. I mean, they have to get *something*."

"But how?"

Nilly nodded slowly and said, "Exactly. How? That's the question."

"I think only the wisest person I know can answer that one."

"Don't I know it," Nilly said. "But you're going to need to give me a little time to think, my dear Lisa."

"I . . . um, wasn't thinking of you, Nilly."

He finally looked up at her. "Not me?" He made a face. "Oh, right. You mean Doctor Proctor?"

Lisa shook her head, held out her hand to him, and pulled him out of his snow pit.

"THANKS FOR ASKING me, Lisa, but that's a tough question," Juliette said, stirring the porridge. "So, what you're saying is that either a kid's parents need to spend ten thousand crowns on Christmas presents or else they can't buy any Christmas presents at all?"

"Yes!" Lisa said. "And they're not allowed to eat Christmas dinner, either. Or have a Christmas tree. Or an Advent calendar. Or go caroling. Or anything that has anything to do with Christmas!"

"Hmm," Juliette said, lost in thought, and gazed

out the kitchen window at Doctor Proctor, who was shoveling the front walkway.

"What if the kids could just get a small present," Lisa said. "Just something to make the day special, something to look forward to."

"She doesn't really mean a super-tiny present, though," Nilly said. "Maybe something like a new PlayStation or a drone with a camera would be enough, though. Right?"

"No!" Lisa said. "I mean something small. A pair of mittens, a book, a . . ."

"Boooriiing!" Nilly pulled his cheeks down with both hands so the red under his eyes was visible.

Juliette opened the window and called, "Victor! The porridge will be ready in a minute!"

Doctor Proctor held up his hands in exasperation and gestured at how much snow he still had left to shovel. Juliette shrugged and shut the window.

"You guys need to go talk to the king," she said.

"He's the one who sold Christmas, so maybe he knows how to get it back."

"Why would the king even sell Christmas?"

"He needs money to fix up the basement of the palace," Nilly said. He was sitting up on the kitchen counter and watching Doctor Proctor, who had set down his snow shovel and was scratching his head and looking at the gate.

"How do you know that?" Lisa asked.

"I read it," Nilly said.

"Where?"

"In the bathroom."

"I mean, where did it *say* that?"

"In a magazine, one of those homes-of-the-rich-and-famous articles. The king has a reaaaaally big basement, but he has mold. In the basement, I mean. So he has to renovate the whole shebang."

Lisa scrunched up one eye. "Can I see this article, Nilly?"

"No, it's . . . uh, used up."

"You can't *use* up reading material, silly!"

"I did say that I was in the bathroom when I read it. It got used to . . . well, you know."

Lisa made a face. "You use magazines as toilet paper?"

"Yup, and I don't recommend it," Nilly said, squirming. "They're stiff and too glossy. My mom doesn't want to spend money on toilet paper. She says we have to save up ten thousand crowns so that she can go shopping so we qualify for Christmas membership."

Out the window Nilly saw Doctor Proctor suddenly smile and then pull a familiar little Baggie out of the pocket of his blue lab coat.

"Poor Nilly," Juliette said.

Then she looked out the window to see what Nilly was looking at. She cocked her head to the side. Doctor Proctor poured a little of the powder into his mouth and then bent over with his hands on his knees and his lab coat pulled up over his bottom, which was aimed at the gate.

"Who knew the King of Norway even owned Christmas?" Lisa said.

"Maybe he had a deed of registration," Juliette said.

"What's a deed of registration?"

"If you acquire something very big and expensive, like a house or an entire forest, you can go to the registration office, which will write up an official document verifying that you are the owner of that house or forest so that no one else can just come say 'Hey, that's mine!' And then the registration office keeps a copy of that document in case you happen to lose yours and someone comes and says that they own your house or your forest."

"That's smart!" Lisa exclaimed. There was a bang outside the window.

"Supersmart," Nilly said, and pointed. "He just used fart powder."

Doctor Proctor straightened up and turned

around to see how it had worked. Fart powder had proven to be an invention that could be used in a variety of ways, and now all the snow had been blown clear, all the way to the gate, with one single mega-fart.

He blinked a few times. Snow was still swirling in the air, and everything was pretty white, but were there really two snowmen over by the gate?

Yes, there really were: two chalky white, completely identical snowmen, although one of them had a Fu Manchu mustache and the other a handlebar mustache. And a police car was parked right behind them with a flashing blue light on its roof and the words CHRISTMAS POLICE™ on the side.

Handlebar cleared his throat and then hawked a loogie.

Fu Manchu opened his mouth wide and then sneezed forcefully.

That caused the snow to start falling off their faces

and clothes, and two police uniforms came into view.

"Sorry," Mr. Fu Manchu said, "but that was a monster fart."

"A truly impressive fartsplosion," Mr. Handlebar said. "It's not every day you get something like that in your face."

"Nope, that's for sure. Yes, indeedy."

"And it didn't stink. Kind of a show fart, the kind of thing a person might wish for, for Christmas, right, Rolf?"

"What I do smell, however, Gunnar, is something that bears a nasty resemblance to CHRISTMAS PORRIDGE™."

"And since we're the CHRISTMAS POLICE™, we're unfortunately going to have to ask to see your saucepan, your recipe, and your CHRISTMAS MEMBERSHIP CARD™, Mr. . . . ?"

"Proctor, Victor Proctor. Come in."

The two policemen followed Doctor Proctor inside, and Juliette was just placing the casserole pan on the table when the three of them walked into the kitchen.

"*Bonjour*," she said with a smile. "Will you be joining us?"

"I shouldn't think so," Mr. Fu Manchu said. "We

came because there was a suspiciously Christmassy aroma coming from this home."

"And that looks suspiciously like a Christmas porridge," said Mr. Handlebar, who had stuck his head halfway down into the casserole pan.

Only now did Nilly, Lisa, and Juliette notice that Doctor Proctor was wearing handcuffs.

"I'm afraid we have no choice but to arrest you, ma'am," Mr. Fu Manchu said, having pulled out a magnifying glass to carefully inspect a completely normal calendar that was hanging next to the door. "And the porridge."

"What are you guys doing?" Lisa cried out.

"Our job," Mr. Handlebar responded. Then he opened a second set of handcuffs and turned to Juliette. "Please calmly hold out your hands, ma'am."

"This isn't Christmas porridge!"

The policemen turned to the little redheaded boy

who had hopped up onto the dining table next to the casserole pan.

"I'm sorry. What did you say?"

"This isn't Christmas porridge!" the little boy repeated.

"Do you think we can't recognize a Christmas porridge when we see one, boy?"

"I have no doubt that you highly esteemed upholders of the law know your porridges. I mean, as a people, we Norwegians are fond of our porridges. There's oat porridge—well, I suppose we usually just call that one oatmeal—but then there's rice porridge, farina porridge, semolina porridge, sour cream porridge, peas porridge hot, you know. But I'm also sure that if you use that hypermodern magnifying glass you brought along to investigate crimes against humanity in general and Mr. Thrane in particular, it will shine some light on the truth. Which is that this is *not* Christmas porridge. Quite the contrary. It's a

Kristi Himmelfart porridge, as traditionally eaten on Ascension Day."

"There's a porridge for that?"

"Yes. It's a little more golden brown in color than Christmas porridge, and also the grains of rice are a smidge bigger."

Mr. Fu Manchu studied the casserole pan through the magnifying glass. "Hmm, there is actually something light brown in here that I didn't notice before. . . ."

Mr. Handlebar took a spoon and tasted a mouthful. "It tastes . . . ," he said, and loudly smacked his lips with a look of profound concentration on his face. "Well, I'll be . . . It tastes like caramel!"

"Exactly," Lisa said. "Kristi Himmelfart porridge."

"*French* Himmelfart porridge," Juliette said.

"Which is traditionally served exactly four months and thirty-three days before the day after Ascension Day," Doctor Proctor said. "Which is today!"

"To be completely precise," Nilly said, licking all the way around his mouth, where Lisa thought she saw traces of caramel sauce, "this dish is called French Himmelfart Porridge à la Nilly. Named for the world-famous little redheaded chef also known for his *Bouche de Nilly*, a chef who was beloved by an entire nation, and particularly by the cancan dancers who flocked around him and . . ."

Doctor Proctor cleared his throat and said, "I'm sure the policemen would love to hear the rest of that story, but no doubt they're extremely busy cracking down on people who are breaking the new Christmas rules."

"True enough," Mr. Handlebar said, and took another spoonful of porridge. "But if you were to absolutely insist that we stay for a bit and have some of this delightful French Himmelfart porridge . . ."

"À la Nilly," Nilly added.

". . . then I'm sure we could spare a few minutes, wouldn't you say, Rolf?"

"Gunnar, I don't think Mr. Thrane would be too pleased . . ."

"No, you're probably right. Yes, yes. Well, we're sorry to have disturbed you. Have a good . . . uh, Himmelfart."

"Umm, do you think maybe you could . . ." Doctor Proctor held out his hands.

"Oh, right, I almost forgot," Mr. Handlebar said, and then chuckled. He unlocked the handcuffs and stuffed them in his pocket.

"That wouldn't have looked good, would it, Rolf?"

"Word," Mr. Fu Manchu replied. "Probably would have earned him a few funny looks."

After they left, Lisa pulled the bottle of caramel sauce out of Nilly's pocket. "You may not be the wisest person I know, but you're the cleverest!" Then she threw her arms around him and gave him a peck on the cheek. And Nilly beamed like the sun.

"But now," Juliette said, "we need an audience with the king, pronto."

"What do you mean 'an audience'?" Lisa asked.

"It's like permission to visit important people," Doctor Proctor explained.

"Important people?" Nilly said. "I'll handle this."

Tuesday, and Now Three Days until Christmas Eve

"THAT WAS A strange letter," the king said, scratching his chin. He squirmed a little, because his much-too-big throne was confoundingly hard and the seat cushions he'd ordered online to raise him up a little had turned out to be made of plastic, which made his butt get really sweaty.

"Do you want to hear this, Vera?"

"I would prefer it if the king would call me 'Court Marshal' and not Vera, Your Majesty," the uniformed woman standing beside him said. Then she re-pursed her lips.

"And I wish you would call me Johnny." The king sighed. "Do you want to hear it or not?"

"I would like whatever the king commands, Your Majesty."

"Boooriing!" the king said. He slumped in his throne, dangling his legs in front. Then he pulled himself together and read the letter out loud:

Dear King:

I, Nilly, of number 15 Cannon Avenue, hereby have the pleasure of notifying you that you have been granted an audience with the

world-famous inventor and snow
shoveler, Doctor Proctor. You also
have permission to greet, exchange
a few words with, and-if you're
funny-tell a brief joke to Doctor
Proctor in the Mirror Hall at the
palace on the last Tuesday before
Christmas at precisely 11:00 a.m.
Remember to polish your shoes and
brush your teeth.

Sincerely, Nilly
Authorized Test Pilot

"Isn't that strange, Vera?" the king said, setting
down the letter.

"Extremely strange, Your Majesty."

"What day is it today? And what time is it?"

"Tuesday, Your Majesty, and it's eleven o'clock."

"And where are we?"

"In the Mirror Hall, Your Maje—"

The twelve-foot-tall door at the end of the hall opened with a *bang*, and sure enough, an entourage walked in.

"Welcome," the one in front proclaimed.

The king had to put on his monocle to see who it was. It was a teeny-tiny redheaded boy. A girl in pigtails entered behind him. And behind her there was a tall skeleton of a man in a blue lab coat, a bow tie, and something that looked like swim goggles. And the king's own bowlegged cabinet secretary came running in behind them.

"They just walked right past me and came in, Your Majesty!" she exclaimed.

"Good," the little boy proclaimed. "We're all here, Mr. King. Wonderful. Now the audience can begin."

He stopped in front of the throne.

"Allow me to present"—the boy stepped to the side and bowed deeply—"the insanely unfamous and unbelievably little recognized Doctor Proctor."

The tall man stepped forward.

"Let me make them a head shorter, Your Majesty," whispered the court marshal, grabbing the handle of her sword.

"Thank you, Vera, but a few of the people present are already short enough as it is," the king whispered back. "Besides, there's something familiar about them. I may have met them before." He clapped his hands together. "Thank you so much for allowing me to meet you, Proctor."

"*Doctor* Proctor," the girl with the pigtails said.

"Pardon me. Doctor Proctor. Now, where have I heard that name before? And where have I seen you?"

"You meet so many people, King, but since this is a brief audience, let's cut to the chase, posthaste. Why did you sell Christmas to Mr. Thrane?"

"Because I have mold in my basement, wouldn't you know it."

"I read that in the paper. Would you mind if I took a look?"

"I DON'T SEE anything," Doctor Proctor said.

The king had escorted them down to the basement, and now they were staring into a room that was bigger than four soccer fields. But it was totally empty. And there wasn't any mold in it either, as far as Lisa, Nilly, or Doctor Proctor could see.

"That's the thing about mold," the king said. "It's invisible. You need to be a fungal inspector to know how to determine if it's there or not."

"But what does it do?" Lisa asked.

"It eats up the walls, and then someday the building collapses," the king said.

"That's true," Nilly said. "Mold is actually discussed on page three oh six of *Animals You Wish Didn't Exist*."

"And who told you that you have mold?" Doctor Proctor asked, leaning over and sniffing the wall.

"The fungal inspector, of course! He came over here one day, asked to take a peek in the basement, and when he was standing right where we're standing now, he said there was no doubt, the basement was full of mold. And that mold is one heck of an infestation, a botheration, a tarnation, a devastation! And there's only one remedy for it. But I lucked out, because he had just so happened to have invented that very remedy himself and that was why he could offer me such a great deal on it."

"And?"

"And I'm sure he gave me a good price by the pound. But, well, as you can see for yourselves, it's a *big* basement. He said it would cost a hundred and fifty million crowns."

"A hundred and fifty *million*?"

"Which I don't have."

"So you decided to sell Christmas?"

"No, the *fungal inspector* decided I should sell

Christmas. He even had a potential buyer in mind, he said. That was Mr. Thrane, of course. He was really a very helpful fungal inspector."

"Tell me," Doctor Proctor said, "what did this helpful fungal inspector look like?"

"Well," the king said, "he was wearing a boiler suit that said FUNGAL INSPECTOR across the back. And he wore a pair of plastic sunglasses with an unbelievably big nose with a bushy black mustache under it."

"Kind of like one of those fake noses with the mustaches attached that you might buy at a toy store?" Doctor Proctor asked.

"Yeah, actually, now that you mention it . . ."

"And what did this so-called fungal inspector say his name was?"

"Mr. Enarht."

"Aha!" Doctor Proctor and Lisa said.

"Aha!" said Nilly.

"Aha!" the king said. "Wait . . . um, why are we saying 'aha'?"

"Think about it," Doctor Proctor said.

"Okay," the king said.

After a couple minutes of silence, the king moaned, "This is booooring!"

"Let us help you," Lisa said. "What does Enarht spell backward?"

The king rolled his eyes and said, "How in the world would I know that, you twit?"

Lisa sighed and said, "Explain it to him, would you, Nilly?"

"My pleasure," Nilly said. "Enarht backward would obviously be . . . uh, tr-tr-trendy!"

Lisa gave him a look that was both disappointed and expectant.

"Wait!" Nilly said. "It would be . . . trainer? No? Chill out, people. Let me see. . . . It would be . . . T . . . T . . . Thrane! Of course! Mr. Thrane!"

"Now do you see, Your Majesty?" Doctor Proctor said.

"Yes," the king replied. "The fungal inspector's name is 'Thrane' backward."

"No one is named Enarht!" Doctor Proctor exclaimed. "He and Mr. Thrane are one and the same. He tricked you! Mr. Thrane owns Thrane's Department Store. He just wants people to spend more money buying Christmas presents. That's why he conned you into selling Christmas. I'm afraid I have some bad news. You probably don't really have mold."

"Why is that bad news? That's wonderful news!"

"The bad news is that you gave away Christmas for nothing!" Lisa said.

"Oh, that," the king said. "Pshaw. I didn't even know I owned Christmas, you know?"

"Really?" Lisa said. "You mean you didn't have one of those deeds of registration that proved you were the owner?"

"No, no. Mr. Thrane came to see me the following day and he and I just agreed that I must own it. Norway is the country closest to the North Pole, and I'm the King of Norway. Given that, I can't really see how anyone other than me *could* own Christmas. I mean, unless you believe in Santa Claus, of course!" He gave a hearty laugh, which echoed through the vast, dark basement. "Anyway, I sold something I didn't know I had to get rid of a mold infestation I also didn't know I had. Plus, I promised Mr. Thrane I'd officiate at the kickoff to his final pre-Christmas sales push on December twenty-third, Little Christmas Eve, at a department store I didn't know he had. So it was a win-win-win situation. But wait! Mr. Thrane didn't have a big nose or a mustache! How could he be the same person as the fungal inspector when . . ."

"It was a fake nose with a mustache," Lisa said with a sigh.

"Oh, right. That must've been it!"

They heard footsteps running down the basement steps toward them. "Your Majesty! Your Majesty!"

"What is it, Vera?"

The court marshal looked flustered.

"The Finnish ambassador is here. They want to lodge a formal protest. They claim that *they* own Christmas. They simply won't accept that the world will not be allowed to celebrate Christmas just because . . ."

"Oh, how quaint!" the king exclaimed. "It's too late, though. Christmas has been sold. Schmick, schmack, schmeck, boom, done, thank you very much! All that's left now is for everyone to do a little Christmas shopping and then everyone can celebrate Christmas!"

"No, now you listen up!" Lisa said in her strictest Lisa voice. "If everyone on the whole planet bought ten thousand crowns' worth of consumer goods, the earth would collapse, self-destruct. Just think of the emissions, the pollution, the scarcity of raw materials. . . ."

The king slapped his hands over his ears and wailed, "Boooring! Vera, throw them out! I want to play Battlefield Finland on the PlayStation!"

The cabinet secretary came to escort Lisa, Nilly, and Doctor Proctor out, while the king and the court marshal walked back to the Mirror Hall to play PlayStation. The last thing our three friends heard before they were shoved out the door was the king's voice:

"Did I tell you what I want for Christmas, Vera? Peace and quiet! Good children! Plus maybe a hot tub for my vacation cabin. Did you write all that down?"

OUR THREE FRIENDS walked down Karl Johan Street, which was decorated for Christmas. Snow was falling in big, fluffy puffs. Warm, cozy light flooded out of the shop windows. A brass band was

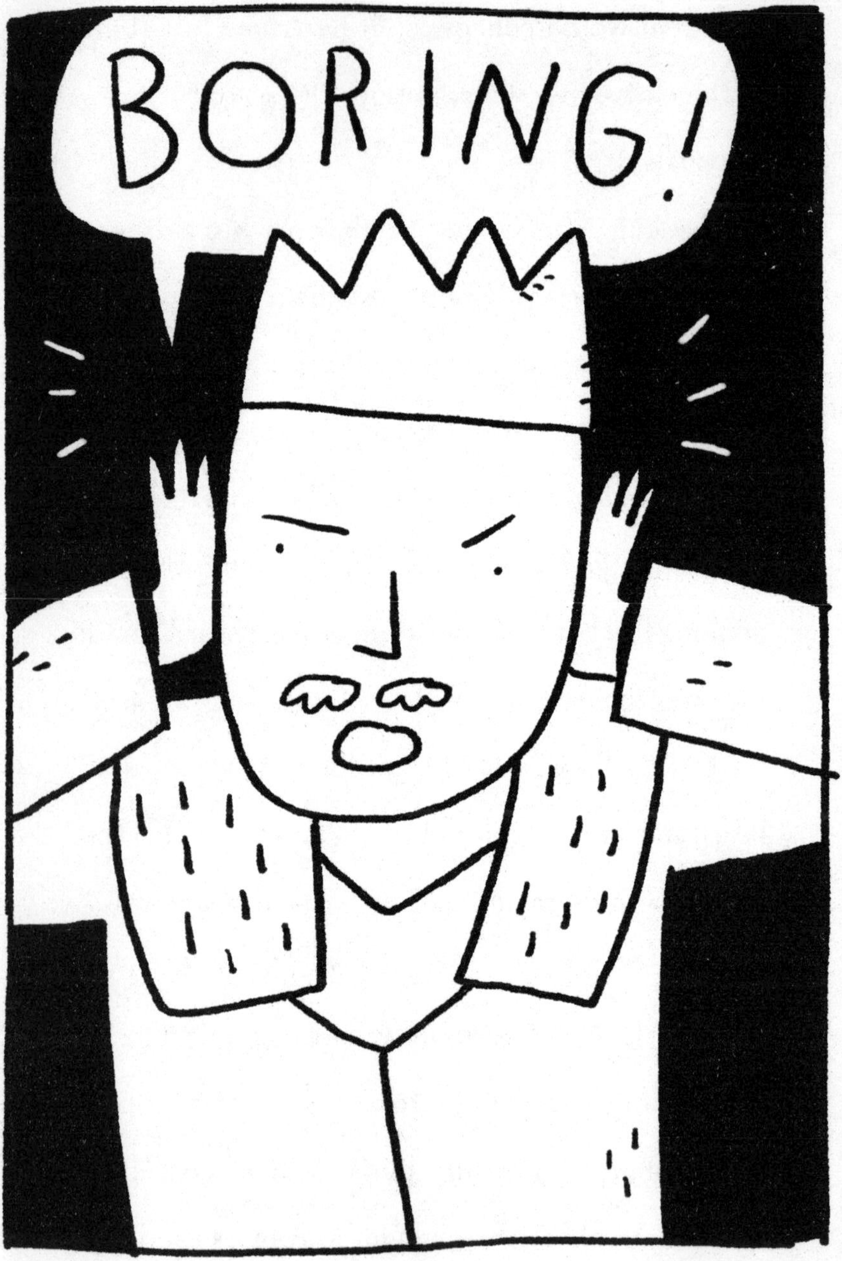
BORING!

playing "Silent Night," and people were desperately running from one store to another to buy enough to qualify for official Christmas membership. The big fountain in the plaza in front of the National Theater Shopping Mall, which had at one time been an actual theater, was lit up in multiple colors so that it looked like one of the jets of water shooting into the air was made of pear soda and another of raspberry soda. And the pool the jets fell back down into was lit up blue, like the most beautiful ocean Lisa had ever seen. There was also a statue of the famous author Henrik Ibsen, and someone had put a Santa hat on its head. A man wearing the same kind of hat was standing next to the fountain behind a table piled high with hair dryers. He shouted: "The most expensive hair dryers in the city! A thousand crowns each! You only need to buy ten to qualify for Christmas membership! Buy them here or inside Thrane's Department Store! Supremely expensive hair dryers. Qualify for Christmas. And they can blow dry hair, too!"

But as they walked farther, they moved away from the lights and the commotion of Karl Johan Street. There were fewer people, not as many lights, fewer stores, and less space between the buildings. Little by little Lisa thought the neighborhood they were walking through was becoming dicier.

"Wh-wh-where are we going?" she asked.

"Well," Doctor Proctor said, "we're going to find the only person who just might possibly be able to help us save Christmas."

"And how is th-th-this person going to do that?" Nilly asked. He did not look particularly tall in his winter hat. Yes, actually, it made him seem even shorter than usual.

"I said *possibly*," Doctor Proctor said gloomily. "Actually, I don't think he can help us or even wants to."

"Why not?"

"Because he's not as nice as a lot of children think."

They were in the city's deepest back streets now. The crooked walls of centuries-old buildings leaned over them, and black windows stared down at them. The protracted hiss of a gigantic anaconda snake could be heard from below the manhole covers.

"Hmm," Doctor Proctor said. "Now, where was it again?"

"M-m-maybe we could come back in the daylight sometime?" Lisa suggested.

"Yes, m-m-maybe it would be easier to find then," Nilly said.

"I appreciate that you're scared, but if we're going to save Christmas, we need to be brave," Doctor Proctor said.

"Fiddlesticks. I—I—I'm never scared," Nilly said.

"Never?" Doctor Proctor asked. "Weren't you ever scared when you were a kid and a grown man looked you in the eye and asked you if you'd been naughty or nice that year?"

"A li-li-little scared, maybe," Nilly said.

"Super-super-super-sc-sc-scared," Lisa said.

From somewhere in the distance they heard the long, plaintive howl of a ravenous wolf.

"We're always afraid of the unknown," Doctor Proctor said, and looked around. "That's why I was afraid of Santa Claus too. But then one Christmas Eve when my father said, as usual, that he was going out to help Santa, I asked if I could tag along."

"You had figured out that he was just tricking you and that *he* really was Santa Claus, right?" Lisa asked.

"Well, that's what I thought," Doctor Proctor confirmed. "So I was a little surprised when my dad looked at me and said that would be fine, that it was about time I found out what was going on since soon I would be big enough that helping Santa Claus would be my job. That was the Christmas Eve when I stopped believing that Santa Claus existed. . . ."

"Ouch!" Nilly yelped. "You're squeezing my hand, Lisa!"

"You're the one squeezing mine!" Lisa said. "Why did you stop believing Santa Claus existed, Doctor Proctor?"

"Because from that day forward I didn't have to believe; I *knew* Santa Claus existed," Doctor Proctor said.

The wind picked up just then. Suddenly, snow started swirling around them. The wind whistled in the downspouts and made the sign hanging over a door swing back and forth, its hinges creaking eerily.

"There it is!" Doctor Proctor exclaimed, pointing to the sign.

Lisa read the black, rather scary letters that said:

THE LONELY TOMBSTONE PUB.

"Wooo-wooo," Lisa said, making a spooky sound.

"Wooo-wooo-wooo," Nilly said.

"And now, children, you'll get to meet Santa too," Doctor Proctor said, and walked over to the door.

"I wish I were you right now, Doctor Proctor," Lisa said.

"Why?" our inventor asked. He grasped the door handle, but the door wouldn't budge.

"So I wouldn't have to be so scared!" Lisa whimpered.

"Oh?" Doctor Proctor said, propping his feet against the door for leverage. "Who says I'm not scared?"

Then he pulled as hard as he could and the door opened.

Tuesday Evening in a Rather Spooky Place. Or ...?

WHEN THE DOOR of the Lonely Tombstone Pub flew open, light, warmth, yodeling, laughter, and the scent of tobacco, beer, and doughnuts poured out.

They scurried inside and closed the door behind them.

"This isn't so scary after all!" Lisa said. She had to

yell to be heard over the yodeling and the noise of people talking in there.

When you walked in, the first thing you saw was an Advent calendar hanging on the wall right in front of the door. It had little doors that opened for each day of Advent, but the doors were covered with wide strips of orange tape in the shape of an X. Someone had written in black felt-tip marker on the tape: CLOSED UNTIL FURTHER NOTICE BY ORDER OF THE CHRISTMAS POLICE.

A plump woman with a tray full of beer steins came out from behind the counter and spotted them:

"*Meine Damen und Herren,*" she said. "*Ich bin Nina.* How may I help you?"

"We're looking for Stanislaw," Doctor Proctor said.

Nina stopped and raised her eyebrows at them.

"Santa Claus," Nilly explained.

"Oh, uh, he's just kidding," Doctor Proctor said. "You look puzzled, Nina, but I distinctly recall this being Stanislaw's regular hangout. I believe he usually—"

"The reason I look puzzled, *Liebling*, is that no one ever asks for Stanislaw. He's sitting in the corner, over there." Nina pointed to the back of the room.

They wove their way through the tables populated by men and women who were slightly past their prime, talking and laughing and saying "cheers" as they clinked their massive beer steins. And when they noticed our three friends coming, they yodeled, "*Guten Abend!*" And after they walked by, "*Auf Wiedersehn!*" as they raised their funny little green hats with the feathers in them.

But at a table way in the back, in a dark corner, sitting all by himself, there was a man who was neither talking nor laughing. He was half hidden behind an enormous boot-shaped beer stein, but as our friends approached, they could tell he was a tall man with long black, wispy hair, droopy skin under his chin, and bulging bags under his eyes like a lizard. He had big blue circles around his eyes, as if he had a couple of black eyes he couldn't shake.

Doctor Proctor cleared his throat and said, "You've lost a lot of weight, Stanislaw."

The man looked up sleepily over his boot-shaped beer stein. And sounded kind of surly when he responded: "And what the Christmas kind of skeleton are you, coming in here and saying something rude like that? You want a clock for Christmas, or do you want me to clean your clock? Or maybe just clock you one? How 'bout a kick in the pants, a walloping, or a wedgie? You want it by mail or down the chimney?"

"Don't you recognize me, Stanislaw?"

"Tell me your name and I'll tell you who you are, you fool."

"Victor. Victor Proctor."

"Victor What-y-what?"

Doctor Proctor leaned over and whispered to Lisa and Nilly, "His memory is starting to go, but that's probably to be expected when you're two hundred and forty years old."

Nilly and Lisa stared at each other in disbelief.

"*Entschuldigen*," Nina said, trying to make her way through the room behind them with a platter of pork chops. "I wouldn't stand right there if I were you, *Liebling* with the delightful, *wonderschön* red hair."

"Why not?" Nilly asked.

"*Die Uhr* is almost seven o'clock." She nodded at a massive cuckoo clock hanging on the wall right beside Nilly. Then she hurried off to a table where they cheered her arrival. "Get out your fork! Here comes the pork! Hurray for Nina!"

"I helped you for years, inventing faster sleighs and gift-wrapping robots for you," Doctor Proctor said. "I'm the son of Doctor Hector Proctor, the grandson of Doctor Thor Proctor."

Stanislaw scowled at the inventor as he scratched his lizard neck, grumbling to himself. Then he laughed, a loud, booming laugh.

"Oh, I'm just messing with you, Victor. Of course I remember you. I remember that first Christmas Eve when you were just a lad and came to the Santa Cave with your dad. And you got to sit on my sleigh. We flew over Akershus Fortress and swooped down over the Oslo Fjord. You laughed so hard you peed your pants." Stanislaw giggled and grinned, divulging a row of teeth where the few that remained were brown and pointing every which way.

"I remember, yeah," Doctor Proctor said. "But I didn't pee my pants because I was laughing so hard. It was because I was so scared."

"Don't listen to him, kids," Stanislaw said, waving his hand dismissively. "He loved it. All kids love that kind of thing." He paused and looked at Lisa and Nilly. "Well, Victor, who are these kids?"

"These are my neighbors from Cannon Avenue. Lisa is the smartest, nicest girl in town. And Nilly is the bravest boy. Well, he's also quite nice, too."

"I know that," Stanislaw said.

"How does he know that?" Nilly whispered to Doctor Proctor.

"Santas have an inborn niceness detector," Doctor Proctor said. "They can tell how nice you've been from miles away."

Nilly cleared his throat and said, rather loudly, "You don't look like Santa Claus, Mr. Stanislaw."

"I don't?" Stanislaw gave Nina's rear end a playful pinch as she walked by, but she didn't care. "So you're saying you've met Santa Claus?"

"No, but . . ."

"Well, there you go." He picked up his beer stein again. "Anyway, I have to get back to drinking now, before my beer goes flat, so have a nice night."

"If you're Santa, prove it!" Lisa demanded.

He lowered his beer stein. "Excuse me, young lady?"

"Prove it," Lisa repeated.

"Why should I? Get out of here, now."

"If you were Santa, you wouldn't be sitting in here three days before Christmas, lazing around, drinking beer and pinching the server," Lisa said. "You're a liar."

"Indeed, I am," Stanislaw said. "A liar, a drunkard, and a ladies' man. And I'm not Santa Claus. So, cheers!"

"Stanislaw," Doctor Proctor said, "aren't you even wondering why we're here?"

"Not really, Victor. I just want to be left in peace. You were a nice kid, by the way. . . ."

"We want you to help us save Christmas, Stanislaw. Have you heard the news? A businessman bought Christmas."

"And now only people who buy a ton of stuff from his store get to celebrate the holiday," Lisa added.

"Really? Whatever. It doesn't have anything to do with me anymore." Stanislaw brought his beer stein to his lips.

"Doesn't it?" Doctor Proctor said, leaning in closer to Stanislaw. "Or is that why you're sitting back here in the corner, hiding? Because you're embarrassed that you're no longer doing what you were meant to do in this life? Making Christmas a bright spot for all the children in this world who look forward to this one day each year."

"I seem to recall that there's some fussy, scruffy, goggle-headed fool who usually pokes his nose in here once a year and tells me that same thing."

"That's me, Stanislaw," Doctor Proctor said. "But this time it's more important than ever! Mr. Thrane wants to deprive everyone of Christmas. You can't just sit here and let that happen, Stanislaw. You have to help us."

"Now, you listen up, Victor . . . ," Stanislaw said.

"You claim you're not Santa Claus . . . ," Doctor Proctor began.

"You and those two friends of yours should just give up on these things. It's no use. Believe me."

". . . but you *were* Santa Claus, Stanislaw. And you could be him again."

Just then the cuckoo clock began to rumble. The pub suddenly went eerily quiet, and everyone turned toward the sound. The rumbling got louder and louder, like a spring being wound up. And then the shutter doors on the front of the clock flipped opened, and an enormous orange and black spotted head with big, beautiful eyes, little Martian horns, and an open mouth full of teeth shot out. The molars were the size of cookbooks, but nowhere near as frightening as the vampire teeth that thrust out like two sabers. The head was attached to a neck that just kept coming and coming out of the cuckoo clock, and Nilly only just barely managed to duck as the head passed over him. He glanced up.

The gaping-jawed, spotted head had now reached the middle of the room here at the Lonely Tombstone Pub, where it was bobbing around at the end of a neck that seemed to go on forever. There was a loud *bang* every time the teeth chomped together as it snapped at the patrons, who leaped up and jumped out of the way, while the clock on the wall cried *cuckoo-cuckoo*. Which was a little odd since that thing that had emerged from it wasn't a cuckoo bird at all, but rather a . . . a . . . a . . .

On the seventh *cuckoo*, the head abruptly retracted into the clock, and the doors slammed shut again.

People looked up from their tables, exhaled in relief, and then the murmur of voices resumed. Soon there was laughing, clinking glasses, toasting, and yodeling just as there had been before seven o'clock.

"That—that—that was a . . . ," Nilly stammered, pointing.

"That was," Doctor Proctor agreed. "Lisa noticed it too, didn't you?"

"Yup," Lisa said, and then sighed.

"So, what do we need to say to Nilly, then?"

"I'm sorry, Nilly," Lisa said. "Vampire giraffes *do* exist after all, and even though I can't promise I will always believe *everything* you say, I will at least try to believe a bit more. Do you forgive me?"

But Nilly wasn't listening. He was just staring at the cuckoo clock. "That—that—that was . . ."

"Is something wrong with the boy?" Stanislaw asked.

"No," Doctor Proctor said. "Something is wrong with the *world*, Stanislaw. When you're sitting in here and kids out there don't get to celebrate Christmas, something is seriously wrong."

"I guess," Stanislaw said, and finished the rest of his beer. "It's been wrong, and it's going to stay wrong. It's unfair now, and it's going remain that way forever. Nothing to be done about it."

"That . . . was . . . a . . . vampire gir—ouch!" Nilly turned to Lisa, who had just pinched him.

"Follow my lead," she whispered. "We need to convince him!"

Then she turned to Stanislaw and said in a pleading, high-pitched, innocent-kid voice, while fluttering her eyelids as if she were on the verge of tears, "Are you sure that you can't . . . help us?"

Nilly took a step forward, made his voice sound

as emotional as he could, and said, "Not even . . . a little?"

"Those are the best sad faces you can do?" Stanislaw said, wiping the beer foam from around his mouth. "Well, I'm sorry to disappoint you, kids, but there's a reason I quit being Santa Claus."

"I think maybe you ought to tell them the story, Stanislaw," Doctor Proctor said.

"Maybe we should spare them. It's a sad story."

"I loooove sad stories," Lisa protested.

"Does she really?" Stanislaw asked, furrowing his brow. He looked at Doctor Proctor and Nilly, who both nodded.

Stanislaw sighed. "Well, you'll have to help me remember it all, Victor. My memory is starting to go a little." Then he turned and bellowed over all the yodeling, "Another boot over here, Nina!"

Stanislaw Tells a Rather Long (but Completely True) Story

"NOT MANY PEOPLE noticed it, but I quit being Santa more than twenty-five years ago," Stanislaw said, and took a gulp of his beer. "By that point young Victor here had taken over his dad's job of inventing everything it took to deliver Christmas presents to so many people in just one night. Everything kept needing to get faster and faster, because people wanted more and more stuff. There were just more and more presents every year. But you know when I really had enough? When microwave ovens came out."

"Microwave ovens?" Lisa said.

"I think you should tell it from the beginning," Doctor Proctor said.

"I guess so." Stanislaw sighed. "Well, I started delivering Christmas presents around the time Napoleon was ravaging Europe."

"But that was more than two hundred years ago!" Lisa said.

"We Santa Clauses live for a long time. For example, my dad delivered a little drawing in 1503 that was a Christmas present from Leonardo da Vinci to a girl named Mona Lisa. We moved around from country to country so no one would discover how old we were and that we also possessed a number of

unusual abilities. Which is to say that people have a

tendency to burn you at the stake if they get it into

their heads that you're using black magic or other

supernatural powers. I was born in Pole-land, up in North Pole-land, in a town called Adansk. There was a lovely beach there where the reindeer could go swimming at night when no one was watching. Apart from that it wasn't such a great place, because there were so many wars there all the time. People kept coming in and taking over the city, and each time they would change its name. From Adansk to Bdansk and then Cdansk and so on. Sadly, late in the eighteen hundreds, my parents stepped on a land mine, and since I was alone I decided to move my operations to the most peaceful, boring place I could think of, which was Norway. That was back in 1905, and I took the ferry from Denmark. Onboard I actually met a guy who said he was going to Norway to take a job as the king. He was the great-grandfather of the current king. Nice people. Yessiree, his son was so nice that I gave him a pair of ski-jumping skis for Christmas one year, I recall. But enough history.

Well, so I settled down in Norway and kept delivering Christmas presents all over the world. I might have been alone, but I was plump, jolly, and busy. I wrapped presents in the summer and fall. Then, on the day before Christmas Eve, I summoned my loyal reindeer from Australia, and we would set out shortly after midnight. We flew for dear life, like a jet, faster than the speed of sound. We were like a shooting star in the sky. . . ."

Stanislaw pulled his pointer finger through the air dramatically to illustrate to Lisa, Nilly, and Doctor Proctor.

"Down chimneys, in kitchen doors, I left presents in barns and on porches, in broom closets and French palaces, on every floor and in unheated garages, in dollhouses, in doghouses, beneath Christmas trees, here and there, for poor people in ragged clothing, even a nice—although lonely—millionaire. . . . We spread joy to the world. And it didn't take much back then: a spinning top, a wooden stool, a pair of gloves. If someone had been extra nice, maybe they got a pair of ice skates. Simple as that."

"How wonderful," Lisa said, enthralled.

Nilly didn't say *boooring*, but he did suppress a very large yawn.

"Yes. I was happy," Stanislaw said. "It was wonderful being Santa Claus back then, you know? The littlest things made people happy, and Santa Claus was beloved by all, children and adults, men and women."

"Especially women," Doctor Proctor mumbled, and coughed.

"Really?" Nilly said, immediately looking more interested. "Were you beloved by cancan dancers, too?"

"Of course," Stanislaw said, flashing his brown teeth and the black gaps in between where teeth were missing. "Oh, women just adored me, as I did them. And why shouldn't I? I was too busy to have a wife and children. And obviously, when a pleasantly plump, jolly man in his finest years with a sack full of presents suddenly encounters a beautiful woman alone in a warm, cozy living room in the middle of the night . . ."

"Did you ever fall in love?" Lisa asked with bated breath.

"I don't want to hear this, blah-blah!" Nilly said, whipping his hands up to cover his ears.

"Maybe," Santa said, staring dreamily into space.

Doctor Proctor cleared his throat and said, "Uh, back to the story, Stanislaw . . ."

"Oh, right, the story! Yes, well, Christmas celebrations spread around the world. Soon everyone was celebrating Christmas, and they were demanding that their Christmas presents be bigger, more numerous, and more expensive. The reindeer and I needed an even faster sleigh to handle it all. So I contacted Victor's dad, the famous inventor Doctor Hector Proctor, who had just invented the tractor."

"No," Doctor Victor Proctor said. "My dad, Hector, invented the atomic reactor. You're thinking of my grandfather, Doctor Thor Proctor, who was the chair of the engine systems program at the college of engineering."

Stanislaw looked at Doctor Proctor with his mouth hanging open for a moment before this seemed to click.

"Right you are!" Stanislaw eventually said. "Well, then Thor built a faster sleigh. And when Thor got old, his son, Hector, came and built an even faster one. Yes, I became really close to the Proctor family. They helped me build better sleighs, and I would drop by their place every year with Christmas presents."

"Wow, the real Santa Claus actually did go to your house!" Lisa gasped. "It wasn't just your dad or some family friend dressed up like Santa!"

"My dad used to work back in the Santa Cave, keeping everything was running smoothly, from gift production to delivery. Right, Stanislaw?"

"That's right. Until he got too old, and then you built me that super-fast sleigh with those clever, aerodynamic modifications so the reindeer could fly at top speed without the sleigh growing scorching hot inside the clouds or breaking up on the turns."

"That was some sleigh," Victor said with a chuckle.

"It was," Stanislaw said. "But then the problems started."

"Yeah," Doctor Proctor said with a sigh.

"It all started when my lead reindeer, Rolf, was shot down during a training flight in Australia and landed smack on a barbecue. Some mighty hungry Australians just ate him right up."

"Uh," Lisa said. "That didn't happen to be in Australia's Northern Territory, did it?"

"Exactly! How did you know that? It's kind of

supposed to be a secret that these flying jet reindeer even exist."

"Did Rolf have a big rack of antlers?" Nilly asked.

"Yes!"

"Then I'm afraid my grandfather helped eat your reindeer," Nilly said, rubbing his upturned nose. "I don't know if it's any consolation, but everyone really raved about how tender Rolf was."

Stanislaw stared at Nilly in disbelief for a moment before he continued.

"Rolf was hard to replace. He was the one who remembered all the addresses, and he was in charge of all the training missions for the younger reindeer who would one day help pull the sleigh. Not that a young jet reindeer needs a lot of training, mind you. They're born able to fly and navigate. But the problem was that in Australia they start shooting like crazy at anything in the air. I mean, you'd think they were giving out rewards for shooting down any poor animal who went out for a little flight."

"They *were!*" Nilly said earnestly.

"Well, it just got to be more and more stressful," Stanislaw said. "And at the same time people were getting greedier and greedier. They weren't satisfied with simple presents anymore. They were constantly wanting bigger, more expensive things."

"You worked so hard," Doctor Proctor said. "*Too* hard. Tell them about the microwaves."

"Oh, those microwaves!" Stanislaw snarled, slamming his fist on the table so hard that the boot-shaped beer stein and the candle both jumped. "I wonder who even invented that infernal machine!"

"That was . . . uh, my great-uncle," Doctor Proctor said. "He thought he'd invented a super-efficient hair dryer, and he did manage to sell it to a hair salon, when . . ." Doctor Proctor shuddered. "That was a very unfortunate affair. For my great-uncle, but especially for the folks who'd just gotten their hair cut."

"Did their heads explode?" Nilly was fully awake now. "Tell us. Tell us!"

"Ahem," Doctor Proctor said. "I think we ought to let Stanislaw tell the story. This was twenty-five years ago, that year when microwave ovens really became popular."

"Everyone wanted one of those doggone machines. Micro, ha! Don't you believe a word of it! They weren't micro at all. Those suckers are huge!" Stanislaw demonstrated with his hands. "They took up all the room in the sleigh, and I had to push and tug

to get those things down the chimneys. We flew
and flew, and I hauled and shoved and sweated and
cursed. I lost more than twenty pounds that Christmas. And I never gained them back." He shook his

head sadly and patted his stomach. "When I woke
up a few weeks after Christmas and couldn't bear
the thought of getting out of bed, I realized I was
burned out. It had gotten to be too much for a single

Santa Claus. I—who had loved being Santa for more than two hundred years—was hyperventilating and having palpitations just thinking about flying off to deliver a single gift. I'd always found Christmas to be the most wonderful time of year, but now it had become something I dreaded."

Stanislaw sighed heavily and stared off into space. "So I quit," he said.

"You just quit?" Lisa asked.

"Yup. And you know the worst part of it was, to a Santa, I mean? It didn't seem like anyone noticed I was gone. Sure, obviously folks that didn't have very much, the ones who still appreciated the little things I brought, their Christmases got a little grimmer. But eventually people started giving each other presents on their own, presents that were bigger and more expensive than the ones I'd flown out to them. And that's when it hit me: I was past my expiration date. No one needed me anymore."

"What have you been doing since then?" Lisa asked.

Stanislaw looked at her dully, sighed heavily again, and raised his beer stein to his mouth. The boot said "*glug, glug, glug*" as he swallowed mouthfuls of beer.

"You've just been sitting here?!" Lisa said incredulously.

"Well, you know," Stanislaw said lackadaisically. "It gets a little lonely in the Santa Cave now that operations have been shut down."

"But what if we told you that we need you now?" Doctor Proctor said. "You're more needed now than ever."

Stanislaw's only response was *glug, glug, glug*.

"Come on, Stanislaw. You could fly again with six high-performance jet reindeer, break the sound barrier somewhere over the Oslo Fjord, zip past sluggish passenger planes and slow-moving satellites, sprint across the sky like a comet."

Glug, glug, glug.

"We need you, Stanislaw. The *world* needs you! And there won't be any microwave ovens, just charming little presents for kids who wouldn't otherwise be getting anything for Christmas. That's why we're here. We want you to help us save Christmas! What do you say?"

Stanislaw set his boot stein down on the table with a *thunk*. It was totally empty, just a little foam left.

"Is that a yes?" Doctor Proctor said jubilantly. "If so, let's celebrate! Nina! Can I get a Christmas beer and some nonalcoholic Christmas toddies for the kids?"

"Afraid I can't sell you anything with the word 'Christmas' in it," Nina called back apologetically. "You can have a nice summer beer and the kids could have some Halloween eggnog."

"Yes!" Nilly exclaimed.

"Yes," Lisa exclaimed.

"Yes!" Doctor Proctor exclaimed.

"No," Stanislaw said.

"No?" our friends moaned in unison.

"It's too late. I just don't have it in me anymore. I can't help you."

"But . . . ," Lisa said.

"But . . . ," Doctor Proctor said.

"Uh . . . ," Nilly said. "Couldn't we still have a little bit of eggnog even if there's nothing to celebrate?"

"Even if I wanted to, it's impossible," Stanislaw said. "After they started shooting down flying animals in Australia, the reindeer elders, who call the shots, closed the airspace over the Northern Territory for all reindeer. And when an adult reindeer hasn't flown in a number of years, they lose their ability to fly. So I simply don't have a team of reindeer to fly me anywhere."

"That's just the adults, right? What about the younger reindeer?" Doctor Proctor asked. "You did say they were born with the ability to fly and navigate."

"That's right," Stanislaw said. "And they retain that ability until they're about ten or fifteen years old. But they're too little and too weak to fly a fully-grown Santa Claus and a full sleigh loaded with presents to everywhere in the entire world. It would be too slow. They'd never manage it in just one night." Stanislaw inhaled through his teeth so it made a sucking sound. "No, it won't work."

"But . . . ," Doctor Proctor said.

"But . . . ," Lisa said.

"Eggnog," said Nilly, who had rested his chin on the edge of the table and was blinking his eyes. "Isn't anyone going to save this polar explorer from dying of starvation?"

"Even if I had the strongest reindeer in the world," Stanislaw said, and gestured to Nina that he was ready for the check, "I don't *want* to do it. I promised myself

I'd never be Santa Claus again. So, I'm sorry, kids, but you're going to have to find something besides Santa Claus to believe in."

"Yes, yes," Doctor Proctor said, pulling out his worn wallet. "Well, thanks for hearing us out, anyway. Let me pay for your beer. And here's a little extra so you can get yourself something to eat, Stanislaw. You're way too skinny."

"Egg-nog, egg-nog," Nilly chanted before his chin slid off the table and he disappeared.

"No, no!" Stanislaw said, and pushed away the money Doctor Proctor was holding out to him. "A real Santa buys his own beer, and at any rate, he doesn't take charity. Thanks for coming to see an old man, but it's time for you to get out of here and head home now."

"But . . . ," Lisa began.

"Would you look at the time?" Stanislaw said, pointing. They looked at the cuckoo clock. "The next time that greedy giraffe pops out, I'm not so sure it won't manage to sink its teeth into at least one of you."

"I think we probably ought to be going, then," Nilly said, poking his head up over the edge of the table again.

"NOW WHAT DO we do?" Lisa asked as our three friends once again stood outside the Lonely Tombstone Pub.

"I just don't know," Doctor Proctor said.

"I do," Nilly said. "Food!"

They started walking back the way they'd come.

"Should we just give up on the whole Christmas thing, then?" Lisa asked.

"I don't know that either, Lisa," Doctor Proctor said with a sigh.

"Maybe Juliette has an answer," Lisa suggested.

"Maybe Juliette has some Himmelfart porridge," Nilly said.

"Poor Stanislaw. He looked so sad," Lisa said.

"Poor Nilly. He's so hungry," Nilly said.

"Shh," Lisa said. "Do you guys hear something?"

"Don't worry. Those are just totally normal wolves and anacondas," Nilly said.

"No, listen!"

And sure enough, they heard heavy, running footsteps approaching from behind.

They turned around.

"Oh, good! There you are!" Stanislaw panted, bending over with his hands on his knees. "I thought about it, and"—our three friends waited while Stanislaw caught his breath—"well, you're my friend, Victor. So I can't turn you down."

"You can't?" Doctor Proctor said, lighting up.

"No, I can't. I changed my mind! I say *yes* . . ."

"Yes!" Lisa cheered.

"Yes!" Nilly cheered.

". . . to the money you offered to give me," Stanislaw said, finishing his sentence. "I'm a little strapped for cash at the moment, you see."

"Oh, right," Lisa whispered.

"I see," Nilly said.

Doctor Proctor sighed and took the bills out of his wallet again.

"Thank you. Thank you," Stanislaw said, grabbing them. "I wish I could afford to wish you a merry Christmas, but that's only for members, so I'll have to make do with wishing you a happy New Year."

And with that Santa Claus turned and walked away into the darkness.

"Yeah, well," Doctor Proctor said, "that's the way the cookie crumbles."

"Yeah, well," Nilly said, "it crumbled, all right."

They both looked at Lisa.

"No," she said, stomping her foot hard into the snow. "The cookie is *not* supposed to crumble this way!"

"Huh?"

"If he doesn't want to be Santa Claus, then *we* will!"

"We're going to be Santa Claus?" Doctor Proctor asked. "And, uh, just how is that going to happen?"

"We need to make a plan," Lisa said.

"What kind of plan?"

"A good one."

"Well, that sounds like a good plan anyway," Doctor Proctor said. "But first . . ."

"But first . . . ," Nilly said.

"But first . . . ," Lisa said.

"Dinner!" they all proclaimed in unison.

Around–Yawn!– Bedtime on Tuesday

SNOW WAS GENTLY falling onto Oslo's roofs. Smoke was rising from some of the chimneys. And in many homes with Christmas candles lit, children and grown-ups were looking forward to Christmas, making Christmas cookies, wrapping Christmas presents, and the parents were telling

Christmas stories from when they were little. But in other houses, the parents were staring blankly into space, parents who didn't have enough money to buy ten thousand crowns' worth of Christmas presents and who were now wondering when to break the news to their kids that there wouldn't be any Christmas this year.

In the blue house at the end of Cannon Avenue, Lisa and Nilly were each sitting on bar stools down in Doctor Proctor's inventor's workshop in the basement. Erlenmeyer flasks were bubbling around them, tubes gurgling, cooking pots hiccupping, and the old record player that was playing a Christmas song, which was surely forbidden, kept skipping. There were many strange things on the shelves. There were balancing shoes that made it so that even the dizziest of clumsy oafs could balance with ease on the world's thinnest, slackest line. There were self-knotting ties that gave you your choice of knots:

wedding knot, funeral knot, granny knot, and of course the ultra-difficult Windsor knot. On the top shelf there was a Mason jar of Doctor Proctor's fart powder and a Dixon jar of Doctor Proctor's super-strong fartonaut powder. On the shelf below that there was a slip of paper that said RATHER UNSUCCES-FUL INVENTIONS. That shelf contained a jar of electric gooseberries, which couldn't be used for anything, of course, a bottle of heavy water obtained from the bottom of Lake Hornindal, which *really* quenched your thirst but unfortunately tasted like plutonium, which is really nasty stuff. Plus, there was a bucket of Doctor Proctor's organic paint, which changed color at least once a day and which he had invented so people wouldn't get tired of the color of their house. Unfortunately, it also caused them to not be able to find their house again. There was an invisible boomerang (you couldn't see it, just the slip of paper that said INVISIBLE BOOMERGANG), shoelaces that never came untied, and chewing gum that never lost its flavor. Pretty much anything you could imagine was in Doctor Proctor's basement. No, actually, it was more like pretty much anything you *couldn't* imagine. And the strangest thing of all was way in the back, in the corner, locked in a glass cabinet, and that was the shampoo bottle with the last few drops of raspberry-red time soap.

Nilly burped.

"Excuse me," he said. "I may have had a little too much dinner."

"That's all right," Doctor Proctor said. "Now, back to the plan. If we're going to be Santas and make sure everyone who can't afford to buy ten thousand crowns' worth of presents still gets presents this year anyway, we are going to need a whole heap of presents. And we're going to need to visit a whole heap of addresses." Doctor Proctor unfolded a large map on the tabletop. "Here's a copy I got of Stanislaw's old wish lists and maps of all the chimneys, back doors, sheds, and cabins all over the world. . . ."

"Oy!" Lisa said. "That's, um, a lot."

"Piffle," Nilly said.

"We're going to need a fast vehicle to load full of gifts," Doctor Proctor said. "But without adult reindeer, we're not going to be able to deliver everything on Christmas Eve. So we have to do something ultra-smart."

"What kind of ultra-smart?" Lisa asked.

"Mega-ultra-smart," Doctor Proctor said. "We have to use time soap."

"Huh?" Nilly said.

"Listen. We start by delivering presents from midnight until dawn. And when it gets light out, we prepare a bath with the time soap, submerge ourselves, and wish ourselves back to the last place we visited, just eight hours earlier. And when we surface again through the bubbles—*voilà!*—we're back at the start of the night and can pick up where we left off, delivering more Christmas presents. We just do that over and over again until all the presents have been delivered."

"That's ingenious!" Nilly exclaimed. "We'll get to live the same night over and over again!"

"Yes," Doctor Proctor said. "But, as you can see, the problem is that we have only a very small amount of time soap left."

"Double piffle," Nilly said.

"But even if we had enough soap, how are we going to find our way to all those addresses in the dark in the middle of the night?" Lisa asked. "And, Nilly, you are not allowed to say *triple piffle* now!"

"Trip—" Nilly began before abruptly shutting his mouth with a *pop*.

"Finding them won't be a problem," Doctor Proctor said. "Right before Stanislaw quit being Santa, there were so many addresses for him to keep track of that I invented this for him." He held up a small, square doohickey. "I called this Gift Positioning for Stanislaw, which we abbreviated GPS, and . . ."

"Everyone knows what GPS is," Lisa said.

"They do?" Doctor Proctor said in surprise. "Well, no one knew it back then. Stanislaw also had the advantage that he—due to his family history of Santa Clausery—was born with a built-in nice-child detector, which made it easy for him to locate the children who really deserved a Christmas present. We don't have that, so if we're going to be Santas, we'll just have to give presents to all the kids, naughty *and* nice."

"Maybe it'll help make the naughty ones a little nicer," Lisa said. "But where are we going to get that many presents?"

"Well," Doctor Proctor said. "I know Stanislaw had a warehouse of presents that never got delivered, but I don't know if there's enough. However, let's see if we can solve the other problems first."

"Like what kind of vehicle we can use to deliver the presents," Nilly suggested.

"Exactly," Doctor Proctor said. "That's going to be a tricky problem."

"We don't have any kind of vehicle?" Lisa asked.

"That's not actually the problem," Doctor Proctor said.

"Then what is the problem?"

"Come with me," Doctor Proctor said.

They walked outside and waded through the snow beneath a starry sky to the garage. Once inside, Doctor Proctor switched on the light. The first thing they saw was a motorcycle with a theater's balcony box as a sidecar. Behind it was Doctor Proctor's big hairdresser helmet that washed your hair and massaged your scalp before cutting a perfect helmet-head cut and finally plucking your eyebrows, ear hair, and nose hair. Behind that there was something covered with a dusty green tarp.

"Give me a hand," Doctor Proctor said. They grabbed the tarp and tugged it off.

"Whoa!" Lisa said, and then coughed from the dust.

"Super whoa!" Nilly said.

"It's a tiny car! With no roof?"

"It's called a convertible," Lisa said. "What a cute car."

"It's nuclear-powered," Doctor Proctor said. "Top speed: thirteen hundred miles per hour."

"Yippy!" Nilly squealed, jumped into the car, and started turning the steering wheel and grasping the gearshift.

"So, what's the problem?"

"Registration," Doctor Proctor said gloomily.

"Huh?"

Doctor Proctor sighed.

"All vehicles need to be registered with the department of motor vehicle licensing, which then grants you a license plate and registration tab. But they said they couldn't approve a nuclear-powered car without airbags, seat belts, and a cigarette lighter. They said that if I drove it they would put me, my wife, all my relatives, and all my closest friends in jail."

"Really?" Nilly moaned.

"This is all according to the Traffic Act." Doctor Proctor nodded. "Which is how the car wound up hidden in here, forgotten under a tarp."

"Hmm," Lisa said. "So the problem is that it's a car and therefore it has to be registered?"

"Yes." Doctor Proctor sighed.

"What if it weren't a car?"

"What?"

"What if it were a sleigh? Sleighs don't need to be registered and have license plates, do they?"

"Noooo."

"So, if this *sleigh* were pulled by a horse or another animal, it would be legal to use it?"

Doctor Proctor thought this over. "Yes, I think you might be right."

"Can't we just borrow Henmo's beagle and tie it to the front? Then if the police see us, they'll think this is just a slightly unconventional-looking dogsled. And if they *don't* see us, we can use the atomic engine to drive thirteen hundred miles per hour."

"Lisa!" Doctor Proctor gasped, looking around nervously. "That would be breaking the law!"

Lisa shrugged.

"We're breaking the law by eating Christmas porridge, too. And since the whole reason for doing this is to save Christmas, I think it would be okay if we fudged a little."

"Rebellious Lisa," Nilly said, grinning from ear to ear. "I like it."

"Me too," Doctor Proctor said. "Aside from the fact that Henmo's beagle would get run over and mushed by the car when the nuclear engine kicks in."

"Piffle!" Nilly said. "Uh . . . um, I mean, rats!"

"Hmm," Doctor Proctor said. He took out a handkerchief and used it to clean his swim goggles while he thought. "I could try to renovate the whole car so that *it* looks like an animal the passengers are sitting on. After all, if the police think the car is a horse, we won't need a license plate."

"Or a camel!" Lisa cried.

"Or a rodeo bull!" Nilly cried.

"The problem is getting it to look enough like something that it will fool the police," Doctor Proctor said.

"Hmm," Nilly said, pulling out his handkerchief and polishing his upturned nose while thinking. "You start by making a four-legged animal, Doctor Proctor, and leave the looking-enough-like-something part to me."

"Uh-oh," Lisa said. "Nilly, what are you up to?"

"Wait and see," Nilly said secretively. "Wait and *see*."

The Next Morning, Only *Two* Days until Christmas Eve!

WHEN DOCTOR PROCTOR woke up in bed, he could tell even with his eyes closed that it was light out. This meant, first of all, that someone had opened the curtains and, second of all, that it was late enough that it was already full daylight outside. This wasn't so strange, because Doctor Proctor had been up all night converting the car into something that looked like an animal. He didn't know exactly what kind of animal, just that it had a body, a tail, and four long legs that moved back and forth when you turned on the engine, so you wouldn't realize it ran on four wheels. But if the nuclear-powered car was going to look enough like an animal to fool the traffic cops, it definitely still needed something.

The daylight wasn't what had woken Doctor Proctor. Someone had snapped their fingers in front of his nose. And Doctor Proctor could feel that someone lying in bed next to him, so without opening his eyes, he rolled over as usual to face Juliette's side of the bed to give her a kiss on the cheek and say good morning.

He kissed something, but it turned out not to be Juliette after all. It was way too hard and hairy to be her.

Doctor Proctor opened his eyes and screamed loudly.

Because there, on the pillow next to him, lay an

animal head, to be precise, a giraffe head. To be more precise, a vampire giraffe head. To be completely precise, a taxidermied vampire giraffe head that was sticking out of a cuckoo clock.

"Good morning," said a teeny-tiny redheaded boy, jumping up onto the bed. "Juliette said we could wake you up now."

"Nilly? What . . . ? What is that head doing here?"

"If you ask me," Nilly said, cocking his head to the side, "I think it looks like it's searching for a body in need of a head."

"And what are *you* doing here? Shouldn't you be at school right now?"

Nilly sighed. "Our Christmas party was canceled because the school can't afford to use the word 'Christmas.' So now we're not even on Christmas vacation, just vacation."

"I see," Doctor Proctor said with a yawn. Then

he smelled the aroma of breakfast and heard Juliette singing in the kitchen.

"I checked on the car in your garage," Nilly said. "With a little paint and this head on the front, it'll look exactly like a giraffe. Well, almost exactly. And I've checked Norway's laws, and there's nothing about it being illegal to ride giraffes on Norwegian roads."

Doctor Proctor rolled back over to look at the pillow next to him again. And even though Doctor Proctor slept in a wool union suit, his body was still instantly covered in goose bumps from seeing the vampire giraffe head from the Lonely Tombstone Pub lying there staring back at him with a cuckoo clock around its neck.

"How did you get them to give you their wall clock?"

"Oh, I made them an offer they couldn't refuse," Nilly said.

"You *what*?"

Nilly squeezed his eyes shut as he scratched inside his ear with his pinky finger. "I knocked on the door at the Lonely Tombstone Pub this morning, but they wouldn't let me in until they opened. Until I explained to them that I was from the Animal Protection Society."

"You lied?"

"No. I founded the society in my bedroom last night, and I elected myself chief executive officer. See? Here's my ID card."

Doctor Proctor put on his swim goggles and looked at the card Nilly held out.

"This looks like a membership card for the Dølgen School Marching Band," Doctor Proctor said. "Only you wrote 'Animal Protection Society' where the name of the band used to be."

"It was the only thing I had to write on," Nilly said. "And now that my trumpet is defunct, it's not like I can be in the band anymore anyway."

"But, Nilly, the Animal Protection Society already exists."

"Hmm, I think you're thinking about the society that tries to protect animals, Doctor Proctor."

"And that's not this?"

"No, no. The Animal Protection Society protects *against* animals, dangerous animals. Which is why I told them that I had recently had an audience with the king and that the society was working on security for the greater Oslo region, and that anyone caught allowing dangerous animals in their drinking establishments would have to be punished with a noogie, having the soles of their feet tickled, or being sent to jail without Internet access. *And* during my audience the king at no point expressed any sentiment that these penalties were too harsh for anyone found to have been harboring dangerous animals."

"But, Nilly!" In dismay Doctor Proctor tugged on his hair, which was even more out of control than usual. "That's nothing but lies and trickery from one end to the other!"

"Is not! I *did* have an audience with the king, my society *is* dedicated to protecting people from dangerous animals, and as far as I can recall, the king didn't say a *single* word about those penalties for keeping dangerous animals being too harsh. Right?"

"Nilly, Nilly," Doctor Proctor said, not knowing if he should laugh or cry. "Then what happened?"

"Then I read them everything it says about vampire giraffes in *AYWDE*. Well, and a couple of scary things I came up with on the fly. So, if they didn't already know they had a dangerous animal in that cuckoo clock, they do now."

"I can imagine, yes. And what kind of an offer did you make them?"

"I told them that if they gave me the vampire giraffe head on the spot, then and there, that I wouldn't report them to the authorities and especially not to the king. And *voilà!* They just unscrewed the whole cuckoo clock from the wall and told me they were actually kind of glad to be rid of her."

"What makes you think it's female?"

"She has such pretty eyes. I think we'll call her Dolores, after the famous cancan dancer."

"As you wish." Doctor Proctor got out of bed and stretched his arms and legs so his joints creaked. "We'd better get started nailing Dolores onto the rest of Dolores, Nilly. And after that we have to get ahold of Lisa and test everything to find out if it will even be possible for the three of us to take over as Santas and make sure everyone gets Christmas presents. There's only two days left. To be precise"—he looked at his watch and scratched his head through his nightcap—"let's see, twenty-four times two minus . . ."

"Thirty-eight hours and twenty minutes," Nilly said.

Doctor Proctor looked in astonishment at the boy with the freckled button nose. "Simple math," Nilly said with a shrug.

"I see," Doctor Proctor said. "But first . . ."

"But first . . . ," Nilly said.

"Breakfast!" they cried in unison.

The Evening of the Day before the Day before Christmas Eve

THE SUN PEEKED out from between the clouds on this short pre-Christmas day and shone on Tommy, who sat leaning against the base of the Henrik Ibsen statue. Tommy had placed a paper cup on the ground in front of him and was studying the pear-soda-colored fountain and the busy Christmas shoppers darting back and forth buying things. Usually they were extra cheerful right before Christmas and would put an extra coin or two in his paper cup. But this year it was like something was bothering them and they had a bunch of other stuff to think about. Like they had to buy *more*. *Well*, Tommy thought, *that's one thing I don't have to worry about.* Because Tommy had a warm jacket and just enough money in his cup to buy himself a little dinner. And what more could a man wish for? Well, he could maybe wish for a Cuban cigar, of course. But Cuban cigars were awfully expensive, so that would have to be in some other life, a life in which he was a rich man. But for right now Tommy was content with what he had, and he figured it was probably about time to go buy a little food. Maybe he even had enough to put a few coins into Olga's paper cup. She was the blind woman who usually sat outside city hall. And then he'd go back to his tunnel, because Tommy was happiest when he was alone and in peace. Too many people made him n-n-nervous. And he'd never seen another soul in the disused subway tunnel for as long as he'd lived there. Besides, the sun would be setting soon.

"You're nice," a voice suddenly said.

Tommy glanced up. A man with a wispy beard and blue circles around eyes stood over him.

"I am?" Tommy said.

"Trust me, I know these things," the man said, then nodded briefly and walked off.

Tommy watched him go and thought maybe the man was a panhandler like himself. So Tommy got up, shook the snow off the blanket he'd been sitting on, and peered into his cup. Yup, there were going to be a couple of crowns to give Olga. But there was something else in there too. Tommy fished the oval thing out of the cup. It was wrapped in red paper. He pulled the paper off. *What in the world?* It was a cigar! Half a cigar anyway, because someone had already smoked the other half of it. But it looked really Cuban!

With a cheer in his heart, Tommy stuck the half cigar in his pocket and jogged over to city hall. A half cigar after dinner, yes! Or wait. He wouldn't smoke the whole thing, just a little. Then he'd save the rest for Christmas Eve, yes!

IT WAS SEVEN p.m. and already dark in Oslo. Nilly, Doctor Proctor, and Lisa had worked all day, and now they were finally ready for the big Santa test. If things went well delivering gifts in the neighborhood tonight, then there was no reason to assume it wouldn't go well tomorrow night when they set out to do it for real and deliver presents to the whole world.

The vampire giraffe head was attached to the front of the car, which had been modified to look like a giraffe. They'd painted it yellow with black spots, put on the tire chains, and wrapped a dozen presents out of things they'd found down in Doctor Proctor's basement. All that was left now was a few finishing touches, well, really some finishing brushes. They had to brush the giraffe's teeth.

"Nice giraffe," Juliette called to the three friends. She had opened the kitchen window and was watching them as they stood by the car in front of the garage. Doctor Proctor had lengthened the legs, so they had to climb a small ladder to get into the large wicker basket secured to the back of the car, behind where the steering wheel and the gas pedal for the nuclear engine were located.

"Her name's Dolores," Nilly called back to Juliette as he petted the giraffe head. "And thanks for the Santa outfits." He ran his hand over the sleek velvety fabric that Juliette had cut out and sewn together at macro speed and in a micro size.

"*Pas de problème*," Juliette said. "But, uh, tell me: Why does Dolores have a cuckoo clock around her neck?"

"Because giraffes don't have wrists for watches or pockets for pocket watches," Doctor Proctor said as he brushed the giraffe's front teeth with a dishwashing brush. "There, ready for the test run!"

Doctor Proctor climbed up the ladder and sat down behind the wheel on the giraffe's back. Lisa and Nilly followed and sat down on either side of him on the sheepskin rug Doctor Proctor had spread over the seats so they wouldn't get too cold.

"Do you know what, Doctor Proctor?" Nilly said. "I should actually be the one to drive Dolores. After all, I am the only authorized test pilot in this car."

"You're a test pilot for *me*," Doctor Proctor said with a chuckle. "So I decide."

"Let's go!" Lisa said.

"Righty-o," Doctor Proctor said, and pushed the button that said NUCLEAR REACTOR.

The engine made a crackling sound. He *very* cautiously pushed on the gas pedal. Dolores's hooves started moving and the snow chains on the tires started jingling as they rolled out the gate onto Cannon Avenue.

"First stop is number one Lilly-of-the-Valley Way," announced Lisa, who had been tasked with reading from Stanislaw's old notes. "Just follow the Gift Positioning for Stanislaw, Doctor."

They drove so slowly through the quiet residential streets that Nilly complained and moaned and pretended to suppress one yawn after another. After a while they stopped in front of a green house.

"According to the notes, an elderly married couple live here. They wrote a note wishing for a pair of slippers for Christmas," Lisa said.

"Here," Doctor Proctor said, holding up a package. "Juliette wrapped my felted wool slippers."

"We're giving them *used* slippers?" Nilly asked.

"Well," Doctor Proctor said, "they didn't specify *new* slippers, and we can't afford to buy new things for the whole world. And this is a good place to start the test, because according to Stanislaw's notes, this couple is so hard of hearing that Nilly can make quite a racket in the chimney without them hearing anything. Are we sure they're not burning a fire in the fireplace?"

"Yep. No smoke from the chimney," Lisa said.

"Good. Ready, Nilly?"

Nilly had stuck a teaspoon down into the bag of fart powder, and now he popped it into his mouth.

"Yum!" he said.

"I gave it a new flavor," Doctor Proctor said, clearly proud. "Cardamomamon."

"Cardamomamamunum?" Lisa repeated.

"No. Cardamomamon, a blend of cardamom and cinnamon. Tastes a bit like chai."

"Three," Nilly said, ". . . two, one. Fart!"

There was a bang. A small cloud of sheep fur and sawdust rose from the car seat, and Nilly was gone.

Lisa squinted into the darkness and saw that her diminutive friend had landed atop the roof of the green house. Now he crawled up the side of the chimney and then disappeared.

INSIDE THE CHIMNEY Nilly propped his feet and hands out to the sides so he looked like a starfish. He cautiously inched his way down. He wasn't so afraid of falling, because he still had enough gas in his gut for a fart strong enough to slow his fall. But they'd agreed that it was important for him not to make any more farting noise than necessary. Besides, the chimney had suddenly grown tighter, so tight that there was no longer any danger of his falling. Yes, so tight in fact that he had to bring his arms in against his body to squeeze his way downward.

He huffed and puffed and pushed his way down. No wonder Stanislaw hadn't managed to deliver slippers here. A Santa belly wouldn't help you get down this chimney. This was a job for a nicely mini Nilly belly!

And boy was it dark.

When Nilly's head bumped the side and the chimney made a hollow sound, he suddenly realized he wasn't in a chimney anymore. This was a stovepipe. No wonder it was a tight fit!

And as if that wasn't enough, he'd reached a bend in the pipe. He managed to push himself halfway through the bend, but—*oof!*—he was stuck. He tried to keep going. He twisted and wriggled, but nothing helped. Nilly decided to crawl a little way back up the pipe and then regroup, but when he tried, he couldn't move that way either. He was wedged in tight, like a cork.

Don't panic, Nilly thought. *Just stay completely calm and don't think about things like not being able to breathe or a carnivorous soot rat or the people who live here deciding it's chilly out so they're going to fire up the woodstove.*

Which is when the panic set in. Nilly screamed

and yelled and kicked and pounded on the inside of the stovepipe.

After he'd done that for a while, he took a break. And realized that if he could only slip his backpack off, his problem would be solved. He exhaled all the air from his lungs, to make himself a little skinnier, and then, sure enough, he was able to squirm his way out of the backpack straps. And then, *voilà*, he managed to wriggle through the bend in the pipe, and then there was more room. A little more wriggling and the pipe widened and he saw light. His feet came to rest on what he figured was the bottom of the woodstove. Nilly squatted down. He was inside a woodstove with a glass door. On the other side of the room he saw a big Christmas tree with the Christmas lights turned on, the backs of two armchairs each with a little gray hair poking up over the edge, and a TV that was on. On the TV a reporter was standing between the fountain and the

Henrik Ibsen statue outside the National Theater Shopping Mall.

"With Christmas Eve fast approaching," she said, "last-minute holiday shoppers are out in droves. One retailer in particular—Thrane Inc.—reports that Christmas sales figures have been through the roof this year. The company urges shoppers to remember to run out and buy something expensive right now, before it's too late, because in order to qualify for Christmas membership . . ."

Nilly tried to open the door on the front of the woodstove but realized it was held closed by a handle on the outside. He tapped on the glass door with his index finger.

"Hello!" he yelled. "Hello? Could somebody open this door?"

But the tufts of gray hair didn't move.

"Hello? It's Santa Claus! You guys might not believe in me, but could you still help me out?"

Still no one moved.

"Oh, for yuletide's sake!" Nilly shouted. "Here I come, bringing Christmas presents and stuff!" He was so angry he was jumping up and down inside the woodstove. "Slippers! Slippers! Slippers!"

No response. He gave up. Maybe they were dead. Maybe they'd had strokes or infected each other with a nasty pneumonia, died, and now they'd been sitting in front of the TV for days or weeks while the phone rang and relatives knocked on the door and left again. But, no, they probably weren't dead, because one of them was changing the TV channel now. First to a channel where they watched a bunch of Chinese people run in and out of a department store with their arms piled high with wrapped presents. Then to a channel where the king regarded the microphone being held up in front of him somberly before beginning to speak.

"I have just come from a meeting with the Finnish

president, and he is extremely angry at Norway," the king began. "He claims that Finland is the true owner of Christmas, not Norway, and he threatened us."

"How did the Finnish president threaten Norway?" the reporter asked.

"He . . . uh, sounded very threatening. And he also had a very threatening look on his face. Kind of like . . ."

The king lowered his eyebrows and the corners of his mouth, but Nilly thought it actually made him look more tired than threatening.

"Exactly what did the Finnish president say?" the reporter asked.

"How the heck should I know? I can't really speak Finnish. I can only count a little." The king cleared his throat and started counting, "*Yxi, kaxi . . . uh, trixie.*"

Nilly sighed. This was only a test run right now, but if they were going to deliver millions of presents on Christmas Eve, they couldn't spend this much time on each one. He set the wrapped slippers down in the oven, hoped that they would notice the gift before they lit their next fire, and then he climbed back up the stovepipe. And got stuck in the bend again. It was the Santa outfit. It was too thick. Nilly crawled back down into the oven again, unbuttoned the suit, and pulled it off. He was about to climb back up the stovepipe again when he spotted an old gray-haired man standing in the middle of the living room staring at him with his mouth hanging open and a coffeepot in his hand.

"Magda," the man said, "there's a naked boy in the woodstove."

"Yes, yes, Alf," an old woman's voice replied from the chair that still had a gray tuft. "You need to remember to take your medicine, you know. Did you get the coffee?" The man looked at Nilly, then sighed, turned around, and walked back toward the TV with small, shuffling steps.

"WHAT TOOK YOU so long?" Doctor Proctor asked as Nilly tumbled onto the sheepskin beside him.

"And why are you naked?" Lisa asked.

"L-l-long story," Nilly said, shivering as he pulled on his Santa outfit. "What's the next stop?"

"Number nine Spitsburpen Drive," Doctor Proctor said, and stepped on the atomic pedal.

This time Doctor Proctor pushed just a smidge harder on the gas pedal, and they *whoosh*ed through the darkness. They took a shortcut over a field and through some woods with snow-laden branches. Then they came out onto a road again as it began climbing toward the houses up on Spitsburpen. But the fog had come in, and the higher they went, the thicker it became. Finally they could hardly see anything ahead of them.

"I can't see any house numbers," Lisa said.

"I can't even see any *houses*," Nilly said.

"Some jet reindeer would have been nice right about now," Doctor Proctor said. "They can find their way in any kind of weather."

"Maybe that's number nine over there?" Nilly said, pointing to a large white house they could just barely make out through the sea of fog. They heard boys' voices hollering and laughing from inside the house.

"What makes you think that specific house is number nine?" Lisa asked.

"I don't know," Nilly said. "Maybe because we hear boys' voices and it says on this gift that it's for a boy named Ola?" Nilly said, holding up his hand. But Lisa didn't see anything in Nilly's hand, just a red ribbon with a tag that looked like it was dangling in thin air next to his hand.

"Is that . . . ?" She reached her hand out and felt her fingers bump into whatever he was holding.

"Yes," Doctor Proctor said. "It's the invisible boomerang. And we're going to have to hope that Ola lives here. If not, then some other boy will be the lucky one. Hop to it!"

Nilly helped himself to another spoonful of fart powder, felt the delightful tickle in his belly, bent his knees, aimed at the chimney, which he could just barely make out through the fog, counted to three, and—*bang!*—an air stream erupted from his backside and he lifted off the seat. He hit perfectly, right next to the chimney, and climbed up it and then down into it. Luckily, this time the chimney was big and wide the whole way down. In fact, it was so wide that Nilly practically had to do the splits to reach the sides with his feet. As he approached the light beneath him, he heard boys' voices coming from the living room.

". . . and we're going to win the big snowman contest this year with Dad, oh yeah!"

"Heh-heh-heh. Yeah, because he rented a bulldozer."

"A bulldozer?" a girl's voice said. "But you're not allowed to use anything other than your hands in the big snowman contest!"

Then the boys' voices again.

"Duh. That's why we're going to build the snowman tonight when no one's watching, bonehead."

"And our snowman will be so huge that no one else will have a chance! Especially not you, blockhead."

"And if you say a word about the bulldozer to anyone, then we're going to crush you, knucklehead."

Nilly thought there was something weirdly familiar about those voices. But there wasn't time to think about that now. He would just have to drop the present down into the fireplace from here and get away before anyone noticed him. Nilly tossed the boomerang and had started climbing back up when it occurred to him what boomerangs did. You threw them and then they curved around and came back to you. Nilly had only just finished thinking that thought when he felt something hard and invisible *thwack* into his knucklehead. Or blockhead. Or bonehead. Regardless, he lost his grip and fell. And fell.

Nilly landed on something soft. He coughed and spit. And realized he was lying in a massive pile of ash. Then he heard laughter and someone screaming bloody murder. And when he looked out at the kids who were all staring at the fireplace, he realized why their voices had sounded so familiar.

"Look. It's the dwarf!" Truls exclaimed.

"Hey, you weren't invited to our Christmas party!" Trym yelled.

"You're not even a member of Christmas, you penny-pinching cheapskate! Get him!"

Nilly looked out at the other kids in the living room. They stared back at him. Truls and Trym started for him.

"We're going to crush you now, you cranberry!"

Truls laughed. "And serve you with our Christmas dinner!" snarled Trym.

"Yeah," Truls taunted. "The roast pig won't have an apple in its mouth this year; it'll have a dwarf!"

Nilly watched the twins waddling closer. They were very big for their age. And really ghastly to have such pleasant names as Truls and Trym. And Nilly didn't have much time at all if he didn't want to end up as the garnish for their Christmas meal. He fumbled around in the ash. His fingers found what they were looking for. He looked down, saw nothing, and threw the nothing at the twins.

"Ow!" Truls howled, grabbing his forehead. "What was that?"

Nilly felt the invisible boomerang return to his hand and threw it again, harder this time.

"Ow, ow!" Trym cried, falling on his butt and grabbing his nose. "Daddy!" he wailed. "That dwarf is mean!"

"What's going on in here?" a voice roared. "What kind of Cinderella are you? Are you attacking my boys, kid?"

"They attacked me." Nilly coughed and looked down at his Santa suit, which was now more black than red.

"He's lying, Daddy!"

"Yes, Daddy! He came down the chimney and threw something at us."

"Get him, Daddy!"

Mr. Thrane took a step toward Nilly, but stopped. "What exactly did he throw?"

"I dunno, Daddy! It was something invisible!"

"Hmm." Mr. Thrane took a step back again. "Police! Police!"

It took a few seconds, and then the door to the living room opened and two uniformed policemen rushed in.

"Calm down, Mr. Thrane. We've been guarding the door," the policeman with the Fu Manchu mustache said.

"And we haven't let in a single person without the receipts to prove they're a member of Christmas," the policeman with the handlebar mustache said.

"But this burglar came down the chimney," Mr. Thrane said, pointing at Nilly. "Arrest him! But be careful. He's armed."

"A genu-wine thief right here on Spitsburpen! And he's dangerous, too. What do you say to that, Rolf?"

"Dangerous or not, we're valiant police officers. So I say we arrest this ne'er-do-well posthaste, Gunnar!"

"I couldn't concur more, Rolf. So, by all means, let's proceed."

"No sooner said than done, Gunnar. I'm right behind you."

"Oh, but you're eleven days older than me, Rolf. So, please, you first."

"Let's nab him!"

"What is he doing? Is he eating some kind of powder?"

"Looks like it, but we've got him . . ." The two policemen reached out their hands to grab the teeny-tiny Santa Claus in the fireplace.

Bang!

A black cloud of ash mushroomed out of the fireplace. And once it settled, the boy had vanished into thin air. And the two policemen were black from top to toe.

"Wow, he really ripped a good one. That was one heck of a Christmas salute," one of them said, dusting ash off his Fu Manchu mustache.

"Yup, that kid farted right in our faces," said the other, blowing ash off his handlebar mustache.

"Well, you know the old saying, Gunnar: Whoever smelt it, dealt it."

"What are you saying, Rolf?"

"Think about it. Wasn't that a familiar-smelling fart?"

"I didn't smell a thing."

"Exactly. Was that the only fart you've smelled recently that didn't stink?"

"Oho! You don't mean . . . ?"

"I do mean . . ."

"Doctor Proctor from Cannon Avenue! Did you hear that, Mr. Thrane? We just solved this complex criminal case with a little quick sniffing flatuloforensics!"

"I'll show you what solving the case looks like!" Mr. Thrane growled, and snatched down the big shotgun that hung over the fireplace. "I'm going to go engage in a little self-defense against some dangerous thieves."

He loaded two big red cartridges into his shotgun, gave his suspenders a tug, and then marched to the front door. The two policemen and all the kids followed on his heels.

"But, Mr. Thrane, you can't simply . . ."

"It's not legal to just . . ."

"Shut up!" he growled, and stepped out into the snow in front of the house and aimed his shotgun at the roof. There was no one up there.

"Shh!" Mr. Thrane said.

They heard a faint rustling sound from the back of the house. And then a strange animal came around the corner of the Thranes' massive house. It was a . . . giraffe! And there was a guy with bushy hair and swim goggles sitting on the giraffe's back. The teeny-tiny little Santa guy from the fireplace was next to him. Actually, the girl sitting next to them was the only one on the sleigh who seemed relatively normal.

"Tell me, Rolf," Handlebar whispered to Fu Manchu. "Is it legal to ride a giraffe on the roads in Norway?"

"I can't recall there being anything against it, Gunnar," Mr. Fu Manchu said, scratching his Fu Manchu mustache.

Mr. Thrane stepped in front of the giraffe and aimed his rifle at it. "Freeze!" he ordered.

"All right," the little Santa said, hopping up onto the seat and yanking off his Santa cap. "There, now I'm freezing. Well, a little anyway."

"I mean *don't move!*" Mr. Thrane bellowed. "Sit down! I'm going to count to three. One . . ."

"Excuse me, Mr. Thrane," Mr. Fu Manchu said, "but do you have a permit to carry that shotgun? If not . . ."

"Shut up, fuzz face! Two!"

"It would be great if you could count to four," the boy said, looking at his watch.

Mr. Thrane raised one eyebrow and said, "Why?"

"Because it'll be exactly eight o'clock then."

A strange creaking and rumbling sound started.

"I'll shoot you whenever I darn well please!" Mr. Thrane yelled. "Two and a half!"

"Gunnar," Mr. Fu Manchu whispered to Mr. Handlebar, "we're going to have to negotiate with Mr. Thrane so nothing terrible happens here."

"I suppose you're right about that, Rolf."

"Then we concur. Why don't you start?"

"Right. I'll use police negotiating tactics to convince Mr. Thrane not to . . ."

"Maybe you should get started on that before it's too late, Gunnar."

"Once again we concur." Mr. Handlebar cleared his throat. "My dear sir! Dear, dear Mr. Thrane, don't shoot. I beseech you on my knees, I . . ."

"Three!" Mr. Thrane carefully squeezed the trigger, because he had to admit he was dreading the *bang* a little. And while he was squeezing, he realized some kind of light had come on in the taxidermied animal's eyes.

"Cuckoo!"

The orange head on the front of the sleigh came

speeding toward Mr. Thrane on a long, spotted neck, its jaws wide open and its shiny, white vampire teeth gleaming.

"Bleargh!" Mr. Thrane screamed.

The jaws clamped shut around his shotgun and yanked it out of his hands. The long neck lurched, launching the shotgun into the yard, where it disappeared pretty noiselessly in the snow.

"Hey, you taxidermied animal! That, what you just did there, is also not permitted under the statutes . . . ," Mr. Fu Manchu began.

"Cuckoo," the vampire giraffe said, and snatched the policeman's hat off his head and tossed it onto the roof.

"No, now this is going too far!" Mr. Handlebar said. "On the roof?!"

"Cuckoo! Cuckoo!"

Mr. Thrane, Truls, Trym, the two policemen, and all the children who were members of Christmas hit the deck as the long neck with the giraffe head on it darted out over them. When they dared to peek up again, they saw only snow swirling behind the giraffe and the three people sitting on its back. And an instant later it vanished into the darkness.

Twenty-Eight Hours Plus a Few Minutes until Christmas Eve

THE MOON SHONE down on Cannon Avenue, where Lisa cautiously peeked through the gap between her bedroom curtains. The blue gleam from the light on the police car outside swept across her bedroom ceiling.

"The policemen rang the bell at your house,

Doctor Proctor," she reported in a whisper. "And now they're ringing the bell at yours, Nilly."

"Good luck with that," said Nilly, who had lain down on the bed with his hands under his head.

"Are you sure your parents won't suddenly come home?" asked Doctor Proctor, who was sitting on the floor next to the dresser.

"Very sure," Lisa said. "My mom is at my grandmother's house making hartshorn cookies and syrup gingersnaps, and my dad is at the fortress manning the cannons in case Finland attacks."

"Finland? But they're our allies!"

"That's what Dad says too, but Finland sent a letter to the king, and Dad says that even though no one understands Finnish, some of the words in the letter sound *very* angry if you read them out loud."

They heard voices out on the street.

"Sorry to disturb you, ma'am, but we're here to

arrest Doctor Proctor and your son, Nilly. He isn't home by any chance, is he?"

"What?" a familiarly yappy voice barked. "What's he done now?"

"Just a few small matters, ma'am. Armed breaking and entering, assaulting an officer, and a breach of the Official Christmas Membership Act. He should be out of jail again in a few years."

"Are you sure you can't hold him a little longer? You know what that boy gives his poor mother for Christmas? A headache, *just* a headache. Do you know how many Tylenol 3s I took tonight just to be able to focus my eyes on the TV?"

"Ma'am, have you seen Nilly or Doct—"

"Nope. Oh, and by the way, that dwarf gave me one other thing. Constipation. Here, feel right here. Yes, feel my belly!"

"Uh, I don't think . . ."

"I'm all backed up, wouldn't you know. Two

weeks. It's been two weeks! Just imagine when this dynamite finally goes off!"

"I would prefer not to think about that, ma'am. Perhaps Nilly has some friends that he might have sought refuge with?"

"Nilly only has one friend."

"And that is . . . ?"

"Okay, I'll tell you if you promise not to torture Nilly. I'm opposed to torture, you know."

"You're safe there, ma'am. We're not actually allowed to torture anyone."

"I see. Well, then, her name's Lisa, and she lives in that red house over there." Nilly's mother raised her index finger to point, and Lisa quickly closed the gap in the curtains.

"I think they're going to come over here next," she whispered.

"What do we do now?" Doctor Proctor asked, worriedly tugging on his beard.

"Let's sleep on it a little," Nilly suggested with a yawn.

"*Ding-dong!*" sang the doorbell. Then there was a firm knock on the door downstairs.

"Open up! This is the long arm of the law knocking!"

The three friends sat still as mice, watching one another and listening as hard as they could.

"I think there's only one thing to do, Rolf," a voice outside said.

"I concur, Gunnar. There's only one thing. Um, but what is that one thing?"

"To request reinforcements from headquarters so we can station a guard outside all three of these houses until the suspects return home."

"Suspects? We were *there*, Gunnar. The giraffe threw your hat onto the roof!"

"Sorry. Of course I meant when the 'guilty parties' return home."

The policemen talked on the radio in their cruiser. Then it was quiet for a long time. Then they heard the hum of a car engine out on Cannon Avenue. Lisa opened the curtains a small amount again.

"Two more police cars just drove up," she whispered. "No, *three*! And now they're getting out of their cars and taking up position outside each of our houses. And they brought thermoses. And sack lunches."

"I see." Doctor Proctor pulled off his swim goggles and polished them. "There's no way out, Lisa. But if we turn ourselves in voluntarily and make a full confession, maybe the punishment will be more lenient. You and Nilly are young. You'll have your whole lives ahead of you, even after you get out."

Doctor Proctor and Lisa looked at Nilly, who was lying on the bed, his eyes closed again, and snoring ever so slightly.

"But . . . but," Lisa said in despair. "If we turn ourselves in now, everyone won't get to celebrate Christmas this year."

"That was going to happen anyway, Lisa." Doctor Proctor sighed. "Our test tonight demonstrated that unfortunately we are no replacement for the real Santa Claus with a real jet reindeer sleigh. We would never have managed to deliver presents to all the children in the world. The world has grown too populous and there are too few of us, Lisa. That's just the way it is."

"You're right," Lisa said. "It stops here."

"I'm afraid so."

Lisa shook Nilly.

"Cancan!" Nilly mumbled. "No, no, wonderful dream, don't go away now!" He opened his eyes a crack. "What's going on?"

"We're turning ourselves in," Doctor Proctor said.

"Why?" Nilly asked, stretching.

"Because the punishment will be even more severe if we don't turn ourselves in voluntarily," Lisa said.

"Punishment?" Nilly yawned. "Ha! Nilly's not afraid of anything—getting my ears boxed, wet willies, en-snow-ment. Just bring it on. I'm not giving up. Nilly can take anything."

"If you don't turn yourself in, they'll probably put you in solitary confinement," Doctor Proctor said. "Where you won't be able to watch TV, put caramel sauce on your food, or say a single word."

Nilly looked at Doctor Proctor for a moment. Then he hopped down onto the floor. "You can say a lot of things about Nilly," Nilly said, "but no one can say he didn't know when it was time to give up. Come on."

"Wait!" Lisa said. "If we go out there, Christmas will be lost forever! Can't you give it one last try to think of something, Doctor Proctor? You have the biggest brain of anyone I know, and when you think hard, you almost always manage to come up with an inspired, ingenious, and outrageously outlandish idea."

"Lisa, I'm sorry, but I've already thought and . . ."

"Please, Doctor Proctor, just one last time!"

Doctor Proctor sighed. "As you wish, Lisa my dear."

Doctor Proctor took a deep breath and then closed his eyes and thought hard. When Nilly saw that, he closed his eyes and thought hard too, so hard that the rest of his face turned as red as his freckles.

"I have the answer!" Doctor Proctor said, opening his eyes again.

"And it is?" Lisa asked, her mouth open.

"There's nothing we can do."

"Same here," Nilly said. "Not one single thing. I hope I get a cell with a TV. And that I get the top bunk."

Lisa sighed. With their heads down, they emerged from Lisa's room. They were about to go downstairs when Lisa stopped. She'd heard a tapping sound. It had come from the open doorway to her parents' bedroom, which faced the back of the house.

Lisa peered in but didn't see anything. And she was about to move on when she heard it again. A tapping sound like . . . like . . .

"Wait," she said. "Someone is tapping on the window in there."

"Up here?" Doctor Proctor said. "On the second floor?"

"Maybe it's a vampire giraffe!" Nilly said enthusiastically.

"I don't think so," Lisa said. "I think . . ."

She walked over to the window without saying anything else, because what she was going to say was so unbelievable she couldn't quite believe it herself.

She opened the window.

And put her hand over her mouth in a mixture of fright and delight.

Because there, right outside the window, floating

in midair, stood six cute little reindeer with little nubs for horns. They were stepping in the air kind of the way Lisa would tread water when she was swimming. And they were pulling a gilded sleigh that was floating right beside the window with a familiar figure sitting in it.

"You!" Lisa said.

"Shh!" Stanislaw urged. "The police are out front, so we need to be quiet."

"What are you doing here?"

Stanislaw shrugged and said, "I . . . What's it called again?"

"Changed your mind?"

"Something like that. But we need to be careful if we're going to successfully get you guys out of here. These are young reindeer who haven't forgotten how to fly yet, but I don't know much weight they can handle."

Doctor Proctor leaned out the window behind

Lisa. "Fantastic, Stan! When did you send for them?"

"Two hours ago."

"Australia to Oslo in under two hours!" Doctor Proctor said with a chuckle. "Now, that's what I call jet reindeer. You first, Lisa."

Lisa climbed up onto the windowsill, and Stanislaw held out his hand to help her climb aboard. The sleigh swayed and the reindeer treaded the air faster.

"Nilly next."

"Yippee," Nilly whispered, and jumped from the windowsill. The sleigh sank noticeably when he landed, and the reindeers' feet were spinning like eggbeaters.

Doctor Proctor climbed onto the window ledge.

"Hurry up," Stanislaw said. "I don't know how much longer they'll be able to keep us in the air."

"So, how is this going to work with you and a sleigh full of presents on Christmas Eve?" Doctor Proctor asked.

"We'll cross that bridge when we come to it," Stanislaw said, pulling on the reins, but the sleigh just sank lower and lower.

Just then they heard the front door open downstairs and the voice of Lisa's dad, the commandant, say: "I just popped by to pick up a clean shirt. The Finns are up in arms. When someone writes 'yxi kaxi' in tweets, you know they mean business!"

"We're not interested in their tweets, Mr. Commandant. We just want to know where your daughter is."

"Well, there's no one here, as you can see."

"Let's just check upstairs."

They heard footsteps coming upstairs, and Doctor Proctor held on tightly to the windowsill as he placed one toe on the sleigh, but that just pushed it even lower.

"I'm too heavy!" he whispered. "You guys get away, and they can arrest me!"

"We're too heavy as it is," Stanislaw said. "Come on. We might as well crash to the ground together, right?"

The footsteps and the commandant's voice were very close now.

"Oh, just let the Finns try it! They probably think we stock our fortress with regular old cannonballs, but they're certainly in for a"—the bedroom door opened and the commandant and two policemen stomped in—"surprise!"

They stood in the doorway staring at the open window.

"Did you hear a rustling sound?" the policeman with the Fu Manchu mustache asked, walking over to the window.

"Good question, Rolf," the other policeman said. "And why is this window open, Mr. Commandant? You're not wasting heat now, in the middle of winter, are you?"

"No . . . ," the commandant said, clearly surprised.

"And what is that over there?" Mr. Fu Manchu asked, pointing out the window at the night sky. "A shooting star?"

The other two men came over, leaned out the window, and looked up into the sky. "Maybe so," the one with the handlebar mustache said. "Or a satellite."

"Or," the commandant said, "a Finnish jet fighter attack plane. I have to get back to the fortress. This is a matter of national security! Lock the door on your way out!" The commandant's footsteps could be heard like a drumroll as he descended the stairs.

The two policemen remained at window. Mr. Fu Manchu had taken out a large magnifying glass, which he held up in front of himself. "You know what, Gunnar?" he asked, squinting at the sky.

"I can't say that I do, no."

"That's not a shooting star or a satellite."

"Then what is it, Rolf?"

"It's a sleigh. With animals in front."

"What kind of animals? Giraffes?"

"Hard to say, but maybe. At any rate, they do all have little bumps on their heads."

"Where does it look like they're headed?"

"Downtown."

"We can't let them escape! Quick, we'd better head back to the patrol cars!"

TOMMY HAD EATEN dinner, placed the half cigar between his lips and lit the one match that was left in the matchbox. The match illuminated his train tunnel a little, throwing shadows onto the walls and ceiling. It was maybe a little scary, but a little cozy, too. And Tommy loved his tunnel.

It was cold there, but not as cold as outside. And he slept well on the soft gravel between the rails. And since the tunnel was closed and disused, no trains ever came to wake him up or——even worse——run him over. Tommy had positioned the match under the end of the cigar and was already looking forward to the sweet aroma of Cuba and Christmas when he heard a rustling sound.

He looked up.

The sound was coming from the end of the tunnel. Something was approaching, fast. It was lit up and had bells that were ringing loudly. And he was really n-n-nervous n-n-now, because the only thing that could be was a train! A train running so late it hadn't heard that this tunnel was closed.

Tommy thought his final hour had arrived, and *before* he had even taken a single puff from the cigar. He sighed and closed his eyes.

A second later he felt something whoosh over his head. He opened his eyes again.

Whatever it was, it was so fast it blew out his match.

Tommy blinked in the darkness. Maybe it was just as well, because he really ought to quit smoking. He'd heard since he was little that Cuban cigars could make people see things. And he had just seen a flying sleigh with lights and bells, with no passengers onboard, but drawn by tiny reindeer.

Still Twenty-Eight Hours Left,

but Honestly, That's Cutting Things a Little Close. If There's Even Going to Be a Christmas, That Is

NILLY CRAWLED OUT from under the bed in Lisa's parents' bedroom.

"The coast is clear," he whispered, and helped Lisa out from under the bed. Then they walked over to the closet and opened the door. Doctor Proctor and Stanislaw tumbled out.

"Yikes! That was a little bit too exciting," Doctor Proctor said, getting to his feet.

"I thought it was just the right amount of excitement," Nilly said, running over to the window. "They're driving away in their police cars right now. They probably think they can catch up with the jet reindeer."

"Yeah, those reindeer are fast," Lisa said. "I just wish they were a little bigger so they could fly a sleigh with one Santa *and* a bunch of presents."

"It is what it is." Stanislaw sighed.

"You don't have any more of those little flying reindeer, do you?" Nilly asked. "Maybe you could hook some more of them up to the sleigh?"

"I have more than enough young reindeer," Stanislaw said, shaking his head. "The problem is that only six of them can pull a Santa sleigh. If you put more up there, they start to get confused. Believe me, I've tried."

"Hmm," Doctor Proctor said, squeezing his eyes shut. Lisa and Nilly looked at him.

"Well, we tried, anyway," Stanislaw said. "I'm going back to the pub. So, you guys have a happy New Year and . . ."

"Shh," Nilly and Lisa said.

"Shh?"

"Shh and wait," Lisa said. "Doctor Proctor is thinking."

"So?" Stanislaw said, and then sat down on the edge of the bed. "Does that work?"

"Very often," Lisa said.

They watched Doctor Proctor, all three of them. His teeth were grinding and his throat was clucking and his hair was rustling.

"But not always," Lisa said.

"Well, in that case . . . ," Stanislaw said dejectedly, and got back up again.

"I've got it!" Doctor Proctor cried, his eyes wide.

"And *it* is?" Stanislaw asked.

"Weight."

"Wait?" the others asked.

"No, weight." Doctor Proctor pointed at Nilly. "I'm pointing at the world's smallest test pilot right now. With him as Santa, the reindeer will be able to fly both Santa and a bunch of Christmas presents. Then we use the time soap to give Nilly and the reindeer enough time to fly a ton of trips. You remember the time soap I showed you, Stanislaw?"

"Vaguely."

"You'll need to teach Nilly to control the sleigh, Stanislaw." But the real Santa shook his head sadly.

"It looks really easy, but it's super difficult, not to mention extremely dangerous."

"Nilly isn't only the world's *smallest* test pilot," Doctor Proctor said. "He's also the world's *best*."

"Very accurately and beautifully put, my dear

professor," Nilly said. "Plus, I like super difficult. And I *love* extremely dangerous."

"You guys don't understand," Stanislaw said. "You have to be born with Santa blood in your veins in order to fly a Santa sleigh."

"Don't you recognize a barn gnome when you see one?" Nilly asked.

"Ha! I don't believe in barn gnomes!" Stanislaw said.

"What about a Christmas elf?" Nilly said.

"Look, Nilly, if you have Santa blood in your veins, you can smell out good children who deserve a present. Can you do that?"

Nilly pointed his button nose up and sniffed the air. "Yup."

"Oh, really? And what do nice children smell like?"

"Cinnamon!" Nilly exclaimed triumphantly.

Stanislaw scratched his beard. "Well . . ."

"Well?" Doctor Proctor and Lisa asked expectantly.

"Well, we can give it a try. Come on, we'll go reopen Santa's workshop."

"Yippee!" Nilly shouted.

"We'll run down to the yard and dig Dolores out," Lisa said, and with that she and Nilly disappeared down the stairs as fast as their legs would carry them.

"How did you find us, actually?" Doctor Proctor asked.

"Well," Stanislaw said, "you said the three of you were neighbors and that the girl was the nicest one in town, so I just used my nice-child detection ability, and the strongest signals led me to this house." He looked around. "Plus, I feel like I was here quite recently, although I can't remember why. Odd."

"You don't remember because you're starting to become forgetful."

"Oh yeah, I'd forgotten."

Someone shouted from the yard, "We're all set!"

Doctor Proctor glanced out the window and saw that Lisa and Nilly had dug Dolores out of the snow.

"Coming!" Doctor Proctor replied.

The inventor and Santa Claus walked down the stairs together. "Stanislaw?" Doctor Proctor said.

"Yes, Victor?"

"Cinnamon?"

"What about cinnamon?"

"Do nice children really smell like cinnamon?"

"No. That's crazy!"

"But, Stanislaw, you did imply that . . ."

"Yes."

"Do you mean to say that Nilly doesn't have any gnome or elf blood and thus no Santa abilities?"

"No, but who knows? Maybe it will help him fly the sleigh if he *believes* he has Santa abilities."

"Do you really think that's going to be enough?"

"Well," Stanislaw said, stopping in front of the

door that led to the back patio and then the yard. Through the glass they saw Lisa and Nilly waving impatiently to them. "No."

"No?" Doctor Proctor said in alarm.

"No, but it's the only chance we have left to save Christmas, right?"

AFTER FETCHING THE shampoo bottle with the raspberry-red time soap from Doctor Proctor's basement, our three friends and Stanislaw rolled along through the pre-Christmas evening on Dolores, over icy streets, slippery sidewalks, through white parks and silent woods, over a frozen duck pond, and between buildings that grew gradually taller as they approached downtown Oslo.

But when they could see the palace, the cannons at Akershus Fortress and Oslo Fjord and hear the bells at the top of the sky-high city hall chime ten, Stanislaw told them to turn left.

"But there isn't any road there," Doctor Proctor said. "Just train tracks."

"Yes, drive on the tracks and . . . Everybody duck!"

The vampire giraffe head was snapping its jaws like crazy but retracted back into the cuckoo clock after about ten *cuckoo*s.

They drove along the snow-covered train tracks for a ways. The tire chains sang against the metal rails. They followed the tracks right into a tunnel. A short distance in, the glow from the headlights suddenly illuminated a man sitting next to the rails.

The man was shielding his eyes and holding up half a cigar. "Uh, anyone have a light?" he called to them.

They stopped.

"We don't have any matches," Doctor Proctor said. "But we do have a nuclear fission engine."

"Huh? You mean like a nuclear bomb?"

"Just press your cigar against the pipe on the underside of the giraffe."

"Um, so, that makes me pretty n-n-nervous."

"It's not dangerous," Lisa said.

The man looked at Lisa. Then he did as she said. There was a little crackling and sparking under the sleigh, and when he held up the brown cigar, smoke was coming out of its glowing end.

"Wow! Thank you so much! And a merry Christmas to you!"

"Merry Christmas," Doctor Proctor said, and was about to drive on, when Lisa asked him to wait and turned to the man.

"What's your name? Where do you live? And what do you want for Christmas?"

"I'm Tommy and I live right here," the man said. "And what do I want?"

"Yeah."

"Heh-heh. I don't know why you want to know that, but I guess I want a Christmas ham. Because I haven't tasted one of those since I was a kid."

"Noted," Stanislaw said.

And as they drove off, it already smelled like Christmas and sweet, Cuban cigar.

They were deep, deep, deep inside the tunnel when Stanislaw asked Doctor Proctor to stop. Stanislaw cleared his throat and then said, "Open sesame!"

Nothing happened.

He cleared his throat again. "Abracadabra!"

Nilly, Lisa, and Doctor Proctor looked around at the sooty, blackened tunnel walls. "Hocus pocus!" Stanislaw yelled angrily. "Maybe 'alakazam'?" he added with a sigh.

"What's wrong?" Lisa asked.

"The door to the Santa workshop is right here, but I forgot the word to open it." Stanislaw hung his head.

"Let's start at the beginning, then," Doctor Proctor said. "A! Abracadabra! Acne! Adverb! Aerodynamic! Aftershave! A—"

"Wait," Lisa said. "This is going to take all night. We need to think."

"You're right," Doctor Proctor agreed. "People, think!"

"Okay," Nilly said with a yawn. He had curled up on the seat. "I think we would think best if we sleep on it for a bit." He pulled the sheepskin up around him.

"Open up!" Lisa commanded the tunnel wall.

"Santa Claus!" Doctor Proctor said.

"Spare ribs!" Stanislaw said.

Meanwhile, Nilly just closed his eyes and smacked his lips contentedly.

"User name and password!" Lisa yelled.

"One, two, three, four, five!" Doctor Proctor yelled.

"October thirteenth, 1775!" Stanislaw yelled. Lisa gave him a quizzical look.

"That's my birthday," he said.

"Oh, right. Let's see . . . Jet reindeer!"

"Six geese a laying!"

"Cristiano Ronaldo!"

A faint snoring sound could be heard from the seat. Almost an hour later Nilly was still asleep, and no door had shown any sign of opening yet.

"I can't think of any more words." Lisa moaned.

"Me either. Wait!" Doctor Proctor said hopefully. "Integral variable displacement adjustment factor!"

But it didn't seem like those were the magic words either.

"I'm sorry about this," Stanislaw said. "I suggest we give up, head back to the Lonely Tombstone, and have a beer. Let's leave Christmas to its own devices."

The cuckoo clock creaked.

"Ugh," Lisa moaned. "I'm so sick of that vampire gira—"

"Cuckoo! Cuckoo!"

They climbed back into the sleigh, and after about eleven *cuckoo*s it got quiet. Then they looked at the wall again.

"Well, apparently 'cuckoo' isn't the right word either," Doctor Proctor said.

"Huh? What's going on?" Nilly asked with a yawn, stretching.

"We've tried everything and we can't get the door to the workshop to open." Lisa sighed.

"Move over. Let me try," Nilly said.

They heard something that sounded like the hiss of a giant constrictor, and part of the wall in front of them slid aside. Our friends found themselves staring dumbfounded into a large, well-lit room.

"Of course!" Stanislaw said, slapping himself on the forehead. "How could I forget!"

"The password is 'let me try'?" Lisa asked in disbelief.

"No, it's *møø*!" Stanislaw said. "As in *møøve over*. Get it?" He marched in.

"That way the reindeer can open the door on their own," Doctor Proctor explained, following him in.

"Huh?" Nilly and Lisa said. They stood in the

tunnel for a moment, stunned, wondering if they had known the answer to the question "What does the reindeer say?" Then they snapped out of it and hurried inside before the doors slid shut again behind them.

There was an enormous gift-wrapping table in the middle of the room, with wrapping paper and ribbons. Little robots in elf hats were stationed around it. Behind the table there was a kind of control panel with knobs, buttons, levers, and gauges, and beyond that there was a large fireplace. Next to the fireplace, six little reindeer lay watching them and chewing their cud in a stall with hay on the floor.

"Møø," they said contentedly.

While Doctor Proctor started unscrewing the covers on the robots' backs to change their batteries, Stanislaw showed Nilly and Lisa around Santa's workshop.

"The workshop hasn't been used for many years,

so it is a little dilapidated," Stanislaw said, brushing cobwebs off a stack of wish lists. "But once we get the fire going, it'll be warm and very cozy in here." He pointed to a picture hanging over the fireplace.

Lisa saw that the picture had been taken right here in this very workshop. It showed a long table with little elves wrapping gifts and a rounder, younger Stanislaw standing at the end of the table, keeping an eye on things.

"That shows you how things looked back when this place was in full swing," Stanislaw said. "Those are real elves, mind you. Such tremendously talented gift wrappers. Unfortunately, they couldn't take the acid rain back in the seventies and had to move to the Canary Islands where we managed to buy them some time-share apartments. Victor's father, Hector Proctor, had to invent these robots for me instead. They're pretty pleasant robots, always polite and they almost never oversleep. But they just don't have the sense of humor the elves have. They don't sing sad songs that make you first cry and then laugh, so they can never quite be the same, can they?"

"Oh, I looove songs that are sad in the middle but end well," Lisa said.

"What used to be in that picture frame?" Nilly asked, pointing to an empty frame hanging next to the one of the elves.

"Hmm," Stanislaw said, running his fingers over his beard. "You know, I don't remember. But it can't have been anything important since the picture's been removed. Are you ready for your first flying lesson, Nilly?"

"Now? In the middle of the night?"

"It's best to fly when no one can see you. And since Santa flights usually take place at night, it makes sense to practice at night."

"Okay! Test pilot Nilly the Flying Ace is ready!"

More or Less Exactly Twenty-Four Hours until Christmas Eve—

for the Few Who Will Get to Celebrate the Holiday, That Is

"YIPPPEEE!" NILLY SCREAMED.

He screamed because he was standing in a sleigh behind six reindeer. They had just emerged from a cloud and were once again flying under a starry sky high, high above the Oslo Fjord. He saw the lights from all the houses twinkling below, the streets that looked like little snakes of light in the white winter landscape. This was the most fun Nilly had had since the first time he'd tried Doctor Proctor's fart powder. He could *steer* the reindeer. When he pulled on the left rein, they turned left. Right rein, right. When he lowered the reins, they immediately flew higher. But most exciting of all was lifting the reins over his head, because then they went into a steep dive, careening toward the ground below, picking up speed, making his stomach drop and the air hit his face so he had tears in his eyes. But right now he was aiming at the moon and climbing up, up, higher and higher.

"Watch out. Don't go any higher, Nilly!" Stanislaw's voice spoke from the earpiece in Nilly's left ear.

"Just a *little*," Nilly said into the tiny pink little microphone attached to his headset.

"No, no! You're almost at the same height they use

for the midnight flight from Paris to Oslo, and . . ."

"I can see it," Nilly yelled.

Because way out over the fjord he saw the flashing lights from an approaching airplane. It was heading right for him, and it was coming in fast! Nilly put on Doctor Proctor's motorcycle goggles.

"Nilly!" Stanislaw warned.

"Yiipppeee!" Nilly screamed.

The plane passed over them with a roar. And the sudden gust of wind that followed it sent the sleigh, Nilly, and the reindeer swirling and tumbling around and around as they careened toward the ground.

"HOW'S HE DOING?" Doctor Proctor asked, screwing the cover plate onto the last robot.

"He's really not that bad at flying," said Stanislaw, who was sitting at the control panel toward the back of the Christmas workshop. "But he's really not that good at doing what he's told."

"Now that sounds like the test pilot I know." Doctor Proctor sighed and hit the button on the robot. A red light blinked on its head, and a metallic voice chimed from the speaker where its mouth would have been: "OUT OF PAPER! OUT OF PAPER!"

"Oh, I forgot about that. I don't have any more wrapping paper," Stanislaw said. "I . . . uh, got a little too short on funds to buy any more."

"I can bring some from home," Lisa said. "My mom has a cupboard full of gently used, neatly ironed Christmas wrapping paper." She'd come over to the control panel. It had a bunch of antennae, small, gray screens, and instruments with gauges and switches. "What's Nilly doing now?"

"He's racing the midnight flight from Paris." Stanislaw sighed. "And he's winning."

Lisa leaned closer to the screen, where the in-sleigh camera showed Nilly's beaming grin and flapping cheeks as he pulled up alongside a big airplane and waved, trying to catch the attention of the passengers. But they mostly seemed to be asleep inside the lit-up plane windows.

"Nilly, get away from there!" Stanislaw said into the microphone on the control panel. "The whole point is for them *not* to see you."

"But . . ." Nilly's voice came through the speaker.

"That's an order, directly from Santa Claus, okay?"

"Roger." Nilly groaned.

On the screen Lisa saw Nilly relax the taut reins, and the jet reindeer clearly must have picked up the pace, because suddenly the plane was way behind them.

"I think you're doing great at this, Nilly!" Lisa called out.

Nilly grinned at the screen. "Thank you, thank you, nice little girl, but when you're an elf, this kind of thing is second nature." Nilly loosened the tightly wrapped scarf around his neck so that the ends

fluttered majestically behind him. "I'm coming in for a landing now at number twenty-six Sognsveien to deliver the final present to Oslo's next-nicest child." With that Nilly raised the reins, and the sleigh dove down toward a line of row houses.

"Yipppeee!"

A few seconds later the sleigh hovered in the air right over a chimney while Nilly hopped out with a small gift in his hand and disappeared from view.

"How's it going?" Doctor Proctor called out.

"It looks like the boy is starting to get the hang of it," Stanislaw said. "How are you doing with the robots?"

"Good," Doctor Proctor said, patting one of the robots on the head. They had all stopped yelling for paper and were instead whirring, humming, vibrating, sputtering, and purring like cats. "They've read the wish lists and now they're printing out the presents."

"Printing?" Lisa asked.

"That's what my dad called it when he invented the process fifty years ago. 3D printing. The robots read a wish, find a picture of the thing in their database, and then they make what's in the picture. Simple, easy, and fast."

"About the fast part," Stanislaw said. "Soon Nilly will be on his way here to pick up the last load of presents I have in the warehouse. It'll almost be dawn, so he's going to have to go back to yesterday evening. Did you fill the pool, Lisa?"

"Yes," Lisa said.

"Where's the time soap?" Doctor Proctor asked.

"Here." She held up the shampoo bottle.

"Nilly is back in the sleigh," Stanislaw said. "It's time to go prepare the time-travel bath."

Doctor Proctor and Lisa exited through the door at the very back of the Santa workshop, which led out to the hangar cave. Just like the Santa workshop, the hangar cave had been carved out of the mountain, but while the workshop was warm and cozy and the walls painted white, the hangar cave was cold and unfinished, and the fluorescent lights only just barely lit the dark rock walls. Doctor Proctor had explained that the hangar cave was the garage for the sleigh. At the mouth of the cave there was some wooden scaffolding that was the takeoff and landing ramp, and beyond that there was an enormous spruce tree. Just inside from the ramp there was a little swimming pool that the reindeer usually liked to swim in when they came back all sweaty from long flights. It was still steaming because Nilly had asked them to keep the water in the pool a "comfortable bathtub temperature for a little boy and small reindeer."

Lisa turned the plastic bottle upside down and carefully squeezed it, dispensing two drops of time soap into the pool. Doctor Proctor stirred the water with a garden rake, and the soap immediately started to foam. When the water was covered with bubbles, they walked out onto the takeoff ramp and over to the big spruce tree. Doctor Proctor pushed aside some of the branches, and Lisa gasped. Because the rock face of the mountain plunged nearly straight down to the Oslo Fjord. Doctor Proctor had told Lisa that they'd built the hangar cave in the middle of the side of the mountain overlooking the fjord so that when they saw the jet reindeer slip behind the spruce tree growing on the rocky ledge, they could go up and wait for them to land.

Lisa leaned out and looked up into the sky. "Where is he?" she asked.

"He ought to be here by now," Doctor Proctor said.

"It would be typical Nilly to be out joyriding right now." Lisa sighed.

"The bubbles won't last that long, and we only have this one bottle of time soap," Doctor Proctor said, nervously scratching the back of his hand.

"Victor! Lisa!" It was Stanislaw.

They ran through the hangar cave, into the work-shop, and over to the control panel.

"We have a problem," Stanislaw said, pointing at the screen.

They saw Nilly and the sleigh flying. But instead of the subdued light of the moon, he and the sleigh were quite harshly lit.

"What are those lights?" Doctor Proctor asked.

"Those," Stanislaw said, "are the floodlights from Akershus Fortress. They've discovered the sleigh."

"Oh no!" Lisa said. "Daddy, no!"

"COMMANDANT!" CRIED THE chief cannon-eer on the cannon team at Akershus Fortress, staring up at the sky over the fortress. "Commandant!"

"Yes, yes, I'm coming!" Lisa's father said, crossing the smooth snow on the rampart in small, rapid steps. All the medals on his uniform rattled and jingled, and the field glasses hanging from a cord around his neck danced up and down.

"There's something flying up there!" the chief cannoneer ordered. "Don't lose sight of that jet fighter!"

"No, sir," another cannoneer called out, aiming the floodlight they used to watch the airspace over Oslo.

"Are you sure that's a jet fighter?" the commandant asked, putting the field glasses to his eyes and pointing them at the sky, at the thing illuminated by the floodlight.

"Nothing else flies that fast, Commandant! And the midnight flight from Paris has already gone over."

"Holy moly!" the commandant moaned. "It must be the Finns! And of course they're attacking at dawn, those sneaky people!"

"Do you want us to shoot at them?"

"Of course we should shoot at them! That's kind

of the whole point to having a fortress and cannons and wearing these stupid uniforms!"

"But should we use the missile-that-never-misses?"

"Of course we should use the missile-that-never-misses. How else do you think you're going to hit something as wily as a Finnish jet fighter?"

"We only have one missile-that-never-misses, Mr. Commandant. Are you sure we shouldn't save it for a . . . uh, special occasion?"

The commandant scoffed.

"And what would be more special than a Finnish jet fighter about to bomb us back to the Stone Age, if I might ask?"

"No, sir, I suppose you're right." They all stared up at the sky.

"Well, what are you waiting for?" the commandant asked.

"Um, for you to say 'launch,'" the chief cannoneer replied.

"Oh, thanks anyway, but it's way too early for lunch. The sun's not even up yet."

"No, the *launch* command. You have to give it to me before I can fire the missile."

"Oh?"

"Yes, you have to give the command. That's why you're called the commandant."

"Right, right." The commandant raised his field glasses to his eyes and stared up into the sky again at the thing that was flying high above, so high and so fast it wasn't so easy to determine exactly what it was. *But it pretty much has to be a Finnish jet fighter. So why am I hesitating like this?* Lisa's father thought. Was it because he thought it might be something else? Was it because deep down inside he knew the Finns were nice, clever people who didn't bomb relatively good neighbors just because those relatively good neighbors had sold Christmas? Or was it because he actually didn't like shooting things down? Well, it was too late to think about that now. He was the commandant. He sighed deeply.

"Fire," he mumbled.

"What?"

"Fire, I said!"

One of the cannons boomed.

And a big, white missile shot into the starry sky. It was head-ing for the thing flying  up there, which *had* to be a jet fighter. Even if Lisa's father had thought for an instant that he'd seen Santa's sleigh up there. But who with any sense in his head believes in *Santa Claus*?

"NILLY!" STANISLAW YELLED. "The satellite image and radar both show that Akershus Fortress just shot a missile at you, so hightail it out of there ASAP!"

"Aye, aye, boss!" Nilly saluted and lowered the reins. With that the sleigh arced steeply upward into the night sky.

Lisa, Doctor Proctor, and Stanislaw watched the greenish gleam of the radar screen where the sleigh was a little dot that said *blop-blop* and the missile was a little dot that said *blip-blip*.

"Now he knows about it, so he can just turn and get out of the missile's path," Doctor Proctor said.

"That won't help."

"What did you say, Lisa?"

Lisa put her hand over the microphone so Nilly wouldn't be able to hear them. "I said turning won't help."

Doctor Proctor furrowed his brow and asked, "What makes you . . . ?"

"That's a missile-that-never-misses," Lisa said. "My dad says it costs one million crowns. And the reason it's so expensive is that . . ."

". . . it's an intelligent missile!" Doctor Proctor exclaimed, putting his hands to his cheeks in horror.

"What are you guys talking about?" Stanislaw growled.

"Once the missile locks on to its intended target, and this one has, it has radar that can locate the target no matter where it goes!"

"And what does that mean?" Stanislaw asked. Stanislaw knocked a knuckle against the radar screen where the *blip* dot was already much closer to the *blop* dot.

Doctor Proctor and Lisa stared at each other.

"It means Nilly and the reindeer don't have a chance!" Doctor Proctor whispered.

A Little Less Than
Twenty-Four Hours
to Go

IN THE SLEIGH'S side-view mirror Nilly saw the white missile closing in from behind. "Test pilot Nilly to headquarters," he said. "There's something weird about this missile. It seems to turn the same way I do."

"I'm afraid that's a missile-that-never-misses you've got on your tail," Stanislaw said.

"Wh-what do I do?" Nilly asked.

When his question was met by an uncomfortably long silence, he understood that there was no obvious answer.

Finally he heard Lisa's voice yell, "Just fly as fast as you can, Nilly!"

"O . . . kay . . . ," said Nilly, who thought he was already flying quite fast. In his side-view mirror, though, he saw the missile continuing to close in. "But are you sure the fastest we can go is fast enough?"

Again the silence before he received an answer was much longer than Nilly would have liked. And the answer didn't make him much happier:

"Fly . . . um, faster than you can," Doctor Proctor yelled. "And make some sudden turns, and . . . uh, stuff."

"Come on, Nilly," Lisa yelled. "We know you can do it!"

"Can I?" asked Nilly, who had picked up his pace, but the white missile in the mirror just got bigger and bigger.

"Remember that you're Doctor Proctor's best test pilot!" Doctor Proctor said.

"Yes, that's certainly true," Nilly said.

"Nilly!" Stanislaw screamed. "Do . . . something! You're going to be Christmas dinner in four seconds . . . three . . . two . . ."

Nilly raised the reins as high as he could over his head.

As the jet reindeer pointed their reindeer muzzles toward the ground, they went into a dive and heard the whistle from the missile as it passed over their heads. Nilly's ears popped, and the lights from the houses and streets down below approached. He turned around in his seat and looked for the missile.

"Well, reindeer, do you think we tricked it?"

They didn't answer, but sped panting toward the ground.

Nilly lowered the reins and felt how he was being pushed down in his seat as the sleigh abruptly flattened out after the dive. He pulled on the left rein so they did an extra loop around the city hall tower and flew between the buildings down a quiet night-time street.

"There," Nilly said. "Now I think we lost—"

"It's right behind you!" Stanislaw screamed.

"Aaah!" Nilly shrieked, adjusting the reins so the sleigh shot straight ahead. He turned right at a deserted traffic light even though the light was red, flew up some stairs, under a bridge, through a church steeple where the change in air pressure he created rocked the bells and caused them to ring a couple of times, over the massive Christmas tree at University Square, right through one of the giant neon letter *O*s in the ad for Toro Soup on the roof of the Majorstuen transit hub building. But the missile followed him turn after turn. With every feint and dodge they made, it kept steadily gaining on them.

The sleigh raced up the hillside, toward the woods. The well-lit ski jump up at Holmenkollen came into view.

And Nilly just had time to catch the frightened expression on the face of the ski jumper coming toward them through the air before they passed each other, the jumper on his way down and Nilly and the reindeer on their way up. The sleigh runners gently made contact with the steep ski-jumping ramp, but the reindeer stepped on the gas. Up, up, to the top of the jump ramp they sped and then off into thin air, still going up. Nilly was terrified for his life and at the same time out of his mind with delight and exhilaration. He had jumped on the ski jump at Holmenkollen! Of course, he'd jumped the wrong direction, but still!

Nilly glanced in his mirror. The missile was a

little farther behind them than a moment ago, wasn't it? Maybe the reindeer were a little better than the missile at flying uphill like this?

"Come on!" Nilly urged. "Prove to me that you guys are real jet reindeer!" And the reindeer surged forward in their harnesses and continued straight up. And up.

And up.

The air grew colder and thinner, so cold and thin that Nilly's teeth were chattering and he was breathing hard and the reindeer even harder.

Nilly turned around and looked down. The missile was still there.

And it didn't seem to have chattering teeth or be breathing harder.

MR. THRANE STOOD in the bucket of his bulldozer in the palace park looking at the sky. He thought he saw a comet with a glowing tail behind it—no, two comets. Well, he would have to let comets be comets since it was time to finish up. He contemplated the snowman in front of him. It was at least sixteen feet tall and six feet wide. In short, it was the biggest snowman in the history of the snowman contest, so this would finally, *finally* be the year. Not only did he own Christmas and was going to make a fortune off everyone's Christmas shopping, but Mr. Thrane was going to accomplish what neither Mr. Thrane Senior nor Mr. Thrane Senior Senior had accomplished: winning the gold medal for Oslo's biggest snowman. Big bulldozer tracks ran through the park, and in some places he had bulldozed so much snow that the withered, brown grass underneath showed. There really wasn't much snow left for the other idiot contestants. So in a few hours, when it was light out and they arrived and got to see this monster snowman, they were guaranteed to just turn around and go home again, those pathetic losers. All that was left now was for Mr. Thrane to stick the big carrot into the snowman's enormous head and then quickly get the bulldozer out of sight. It was still dark out, but people would start waking up soon, and some of them would walk through the palace park on their way to their last day of work before the Christmas holidays. And if they noticed the bulldozer, it might occur to them to go see the

snowman contest committee and tell them that Mr. Thrane had cheated. And even if that was true, obviously even the biggest numbskull knew that it was far better to cheat *without anyone* knowing about it *and* win the gold medal than to cheat in such a way that *everyone* found out about it and *not* win the gold medal.

"Bring me a little closer," Mr. Thrane yelled to his twins, who were sitting in the bulldozer's driver's seat arguing over which one of them would drive and which one would control the digging bucket.

The bulldozer started moving.

"Stop!" Mr. Thrane screamed, and the bulldozer stopped so abruptly that Mr. Thrane fell over in the bucket. He stood back up, his face red with rage. "Tell me this: Can't you boys drive a bulldozer?"

"We're just kids, Dad!" Truls protested.

"Yes," Mr. Thrane said. "Little babies who drive like old biddies!" He leaned out over the edge of the bucket but couldn't reach the snowman's head. "Raise the bucket some more, Trym!"

The bucket jerked upward and stopped abruptly, causing Mr. Thrane to first hiccup and then bite his tongue.

He closed his eyes and counted slowly to ten in his mind, wondering how a genius like himself could have produced two idiots the likes of his sons. Because there was no doubt he was a genius. Who but a genius could have fooled the king into selling Christmas? Especially since no one had known the king even owned Christmas. No, there was only one word for something so sly, shrewd, and sneaky, and that was "genius"! But they still needed to stick in this crummy carrot nose. Mr. Thrane tried again, reaching from the bucket with the carrot in his hand. But something felt too tight. It was his suspenders. He loosened them a little and reached again toward the sixteen-foot-tall snowman.

"How's it going, Dad?" Truls called out.

"Can you reach, Dad?" Trym yelled.

"Yes!" Mr. Thrane grunted. The carrot was nearing the snowman's head. Only an inch or two to go now.

"NILLY!" LISA YELLED desperately at the control panel. "Nilly!"

"The sleigh is too high. He's out of range. We can't see him on the screen and we've lost radio contact," Stanislaw said.

"Will we . . . ? Will we ever see or hear him again?"

"I don't know. This radio transmitter wasn't intended for regular shortwave radio but rather high-voltage, strong-current, wide-wave Santa frequency."

Lisa turned to Doctor Proctor and asked, "What is he saying?"

"Santas are born with a kind of radio receiver in their brains," the inventor explained. "That means they can hear anything anyone says on the Santa frequency no matter where they are on earth."

"And Nilly only has a normal radio," Lisa said, on the verge of tears. "Because Nilly is only a normal boy."

"But even being Santa wouldn't help him now, I'm afraid," Stanislaw said, pointing at the radar.

Lisa stared. The *blip* dot was almost on top of the *blop* dot now.

"Only a normal boy," Doctor Proctor repeated, sounding as if he, too, wanted to cry.

"LOOP!" NILLY YELLED. "How do you do a loop-the-loop?" But there was no answer in his earpiece.

The reindeer continued up and up, higher and higher in front of him, but the missile was getting closer and closer behind him.

He flicked the reins, crossed them, clicked his tongue, yelled, "whoa!" and snapped his fingers. But nothing helped. He could hear the sizzling sound from the missile behind him now.

"Møø!" he yelled.

"Møø!" the reindeer said.

"Møø-møø!" Nilly yelled.

"Møø-møø!"

"No, loop-the-loop! Roll! Backward! Uh . . . um . . . øøm-øøm?"

"Øøm-øøm!"

And with that, the reindeer curved up, over, and back until they were flying upside down, pulling the sleigh behind them so that it was hanging upside down in the middle of a perfect loop, and for a second Nilly was sure he would fall out. But then the reindeer were under him and the downward part of the loop began. Nilly heard only the whoosh of the missile, which was still on its way up before he saw the glow of Oslo below them start to grow. The glow became individual buildings, houses, streetlights, headlights, and boat lanterns out on the black fjord. And although he knew the missile was after them again, Nilly thought he might as well enjoy the fun bits of life while he could. So he let out a long, "Yiiiipppeee!"

He aimed at the thing that was lit up the brightest, the structure that was biggest and in the heart of the city.

The palace.

Nilly was going so fast now that the fillings in his teeth were rattling, so he closed his mouth and concentrated. And as the sleigh passed the flag at the top of the king's flagpole, Nilly quickly lowered the reins. The sleigh flattened out and passed in front of the palace at such a raw, rushing, rump-shaking speed that the air pressure knocked the hats clean off the two guards on duty.

Nilly steered between the trees in the park on the

palace grounds, up over a hill, along a footpath, past a bench, over a frozen pond, between two enormous oak trees. And there, suddenly, right in front of him, a white giant appeared, and Nilly realized it was too late to avoid impact.

"YOU SEE, TRULS and Trym?" yelled Mr. Thrane, who had just jabbed the carrot into the snowman's head. He took a step back in the bulldozer's bucket and beheld his perfect creation with pride. Or, wait a minute. It wasn't *completely* perfect. The carrot nose was a *tad* crooked. Mr. Thrane sighed, leaned out of the bucket again and grasped the carrot. As he did so he noticed something out of the corner of his eye, something approaching alarmingly fast. Then everything exploded in a huge cloud of snow, and Mr. Thrane fell out of the bucket. He spat and blinked, and once he got the snow off his face, he realized he was lying on top of his soon-to-be-prize-winning snowman, which wasn't anywhere near as impressively large now that it's head was missing. All that was left was the carrot, which Mr. Thrane was still clutching in his hand.

"Did you guys see that?" He moaned.

"Daddy . . . ," Trym said.

"We see something else . . . ," Truls said.

Mr. Thrane turned around. And there, from between the oak trees, he saw a white missile speeding toward them.

"No!" he screamed, clinging protectively to his headless snowman. "Please . . . don't!"

But missiles don't care about "please" or "don't" or "hang on a second." They hurtle on no matter what they encounter, and—*poof!*—there went the whole snowman, disintegrated into a cloud of snow that slowly settled like a small flurry over the park, the bulldozer, and the twins.

Truls coughed. Trym coughed.

And then they looked at each other and asked, "Where's Daddy?"

"THE MISSILE SEEMS to have slowed down a little. It's flying slower than the sleigh now," Stanislaw said, pointing to the radar screen. "Strange."

"But that's wonderful!" Lisa said, jumping up and down and clapping her hands.

"I'm afraid it won't last," Stanislaw said, and pointed to the reindeer-pulse-ometer. "The reindeer are exhausted."

Just then the radio crackled.

"Nilly to headquarters! SOS! SOS!"

"We've reestablished radio contact! The picture's back," Stanislaw said, pointing to the video screen.

"Nilly!" Doctor Proctor cried. "Where are you?"

"We're flying over the rooftops downtown!" Nilly yelled. "But the reindeer are at their limit. We're flying lower and lower! We're going to crash soon!"

"If they crash, the missile will hit them," Doctor Proctor said. "We have to think of something, and fast!"

"He should come back here!" Lisa said. "No, I guess then the missile would just follow and blow us all to smithereens. He should . . . he should . . ."

"It's no use, Lisa," Doctor Proctor said, choking up.

"All is lost," Stanislaw said gloomily. "Let's go remember Nilly and the reindeer with a beer and a nice memorial supper."

"I've got it!" Lisa exclaimed.

"You do?" Doctor Proctor and Stanislaw exclaimed in unison.

"Nilly!" Lisa yelled into the microphone. "The missile is flying slower too, so hang on for six more minutes. Then crash!"

"Crash?" Nilly shouted with dismay.

"Yes. Crash into the fountain at the National Theater Shopping Mall."

"But . . ."

"And then close your eyes and think about the Santa workshop. In exactly six minutes from now!"

"I get it! I don't know if we can hold out that long, but we'll try!"

Lisa turned to Stanislaw and said, "You help Nilly keep an eye on the time. I think his pocket watch runs a little fast."

"Roger!" Stanislaw said.

"And Doctor Proctor, you're with me!"

"Check!" Doctor Proctor said.

And with that, Lisa and Doctor Proctor climbed aboard Dolores and rolled out of the workshop and into the tunnel.

That little girl Lisa sure is commandant-like when she gives commands, Stanislaw thought as he looked at the time. Six minutes. He glanced at the radar screen again. The missile was lagging even farther behind the sleigh now. He scratched his beard. Missiles didn't get tired, did they? So what in the world would suddenly make it start flying slower?

"WAAAAAH!" SHRIEKED MR. Thrane. "Double waaaaah!"

And the big, fat man had good reason to say that, since he was hanging by his suspenders from a missile.

We Stop Here for a Little Breather

Since We Just Realized Mr. Thrane Is Stuck to the Missile That's Chasing Nilly. There, Did You Breathe? Okay, Then Let's Continue...

"MY DEAR, MUCH-LOVED reindeer," Nilly called out as they flew over the Oslo Fjord. "I know you're tired, but just a *little* more now."

They were still flying at a good clip, but they were getting lower and lower. The good news was that the distance to the missile behind them was getting bigger and bigger.

Nilly aimed for a light out in the fjord that was sweeping back and forth. It turned out to be a very welcoming lighthouse, decorated with fir boughs for the holidays, tucked away on an isolated islet. The sleigh was only fifty feet over the water now. Nilly pulled out his pocket watch and checked it. One minute left until it had been six minutes. He wasn't so worried about the missile anymore, but he was *very* worried about the crashing. What was Lisa's plan? Well, if there was anyone he trusted in a sticky situation, it was his best friend, so it was sure to be something clever. Of course, the problem was that it would be even better if Lisa could come up with something *very* clever!

They passed the lighthouse, and Nilly pulled on the left rein so the sleigh turned sharply and started heading back to town. And there, right in front of them, at the very inland end of the fjord, lay the city, lit up like a Christmas tree. He aimed for city hall, because he knew the National Theater Shopping Mall and the fountain were right behind it.

"Giddyap, giddyap!" Nilly said. "Time to crash!"

"WAAAH," SOBBED MR. Thrane. "Triple waaah."

Because, really, what else could you do if you were hanging by your suspenders from a speeding missile that was heading out over the Oslo Fjord? Well, of course he could pray to God. Because although Mr. Thrane had always been sure there was no God, he could certainly hope he'd been wrong.

"Dear God," Mr. Thrane sobbed, folding his stiff, frozen hands together. "If I make it out of this alive, I promise I will never again trick kings, steal Christmas or other holidays, or cheat in national snowman contests. Dear, dear God. I *promise!* Everyone will be allowed to celebrate Christmas, totally for free. They won't need to buy anything at all!"

Just then they passed a lighthouse and the missile made a sharp turn, so sharp that Mr. Thrane was slung way out to the side and his suspenders stretched and stretched. And right when they were about to start contracting again there was a *sproing*!

"Ho-ho!" Mr. Thrane cheered. Because finally the fat man was being rewarded for all the steaks, roasts, pork chops, hamburgers, Wiener schnitzels, jelly doughnuts, and beer he had polished off. Mr. Thrane's weight had grown so great that his suspenders had snapped! And now he was sailing through the air, free from the missile, free from everything!

"Ho-ho . . ."

Mr. Thrane abruptly stopped celebrating when he realized that he was out over the middle of the Oslo Fjord, that very soon he would be *in* the Oslo Fjord, which he was approaching at a frighteningly

rapid pace. It wasn't that he couldn't swim, but it was the middle of winter, this was Norway, and that water was going to be beastly cold, twenty degrees below freezing at least. The way things looked right now, there was going to be one heck of a belly flop and a few weak swim strokes before he froze to death and drowned. Or, wait a minute, maybe you couldn't drown if you had already frozen to death? Yes, yes, at least he could take some comfort in that, Mr. Thrane thought as he watched the surface of the water approaching. He closed his eyes.

And it turned out Mr. Thrane was right. The water *was* about twenty degrees below freezing.

But that's also what saved him. Because the interesting thing about water that's below freezing is that it is . . . think, now . . . quite right: ice.

There was an ugly smack as the three-hundred-and-fifty-pound Thrane struck the eight-inch-thick ice.

"Owie!" screamed Mr. Thrane. "Double owie!"

At first he lay there for a bit checking to see if he was intact.

He hurt all over, but he appeared to be in one piece. Then he tried moving.

That hurt even more, but at least he could move.

Then he opened his eyes to be completely sure he hadn't frozen to death or drowned.

That hurt so much that for a second he wondered if he might rather be drowned or frozen solid.

The Oslo Fjord was indeed frozen over. Sure, the ice didn't extend all the way to downtown Oslo and the city hall pier, because there was so much ferry traffic there that broke up the ice. But at any rate there was ice all the way over to the lonely islet with the little lighthouse on it.

"Thank God," whispered Mr. Thrane. Groaning, he stood up and started limping toward the light-house. He would sit on the islet until it got light out and then hope that someone aboard one of the ferries would spot him. It was cold, but as long as he stayed dry . . .

The ice cracked beneath him.

No, Mr. Thrane thought. *No . . .*

But yes. As he went through the ice with a crack, a splash, and a small "waaah!" Mr. Thrane was punished for all the steaks, roasts, pork chops, hamburgers, Wiener schnitzels, jelly doughnuts, and beer he had polished off

NILLY WAS JUST passing city hall when he heard Stanislaw's voice in his earpiece. "Nilly! Nilly!"

"Let me guess," Nilly said, glancing at the pocket watch he had set in front of him on the dashboard of the sleigh. "Lisa asked you to help me keep an eye on the time. But I know there's one minute to go until I'm supposed to crash in the fountain."

"You have to do it sooner!"

"Sooner? Why?"

"Because the missile suddenly sped up again!"

"Sped up?"

"I have no idea why, but it's going to hit you soon!"

Nilly glanced in his side-view mirror, and sure enough, there it was, zooming toward him. It would be only a matter of seconds.

Nilly did a turn around the city hall tower, and then the square in front of the National Theater Shopping Mall was below them, well lit but almost devoid of people. And there, between the fountain and the Henrik Ibsen statue, he saw a giraffe and two familiar figures. But there were no soap bubbles in the fountain!

"Sorry, my dear reindeer, but given the choice between having that missile blow us up and crashing, I'm going to go with crashing!"

Then he raised the reins, and the out-of-breath reindeer obeyed and went into one final dive.

Their speed picked up. "Yippee," Nilly whispered

gloomily. Then he closed his eyes and tried to think of something pleasant.

"THEY'RE COMING TOO soon!" Lisa yelled, pointing to the sky.

"But the time soap isn't foaming yet!" Doctor Proctor said, frantically stirring the fountain water where Lisa had just added three drops from the shampoo bottle of time soap.

"Do . . . something!" Lisa shouted.

"What?"

"Anything!"

"But there isn't anything to do, Lisa."

Dear, dear God, she thought, even though she didn't actually believe in any gods. *Let there be a miracle. Then I promise I'll never . . . never . . .* But she couldn't think of anything, because Lisa was actually such a nice person already that it wasn't very easy to think of anything she could do to make this God any more satisfied with her.

"Cuckoo!"

It was exactly six o'clock in the morning, and for an instant Lisa found herself staring into a pair of big, beautiful giraffe eyes and a not-so-beautiful giraffe mouth before that mouth chomped shut around the shampoo bottle. And since Lisa hadn't screwed the lid back on yet and since a vampire giraffe bites harder than twenty great white sharks and an anaconda put together, all—*absolutely* all— the time soap squirted out of the top of the bottle in a looong, elegant raspberry-red stream. The stream of soap was so long that it landed halfway up one of the fountain's jets of water that was shooting into the air, the jet that looked like pear soda.

"Oh no, all the time soap . . . ," Lisa moaned.

Doctor Proctor looked up. "The missile . . . ," he

whispered aghast. He then grabbed Lisa by the arm and pulled her out of the way.

THE COMMANDANT STOOD at the top of the tower at Akershus Fortress looking through his field glasses.

"What's going on?" the cannoneer asked.

"The Finnish jet fighter just crashed right in front of the National Theater Shopping Mall," the commandant said. "There! Yikes, what a splash!"

"Yikes! What about the missile? Tell me. Tell me!"

"The missile is right behind it! Let's count down . . . *kaxi, yxi, and kaboom*! Whoa, what an explosion! It's like ten New Year's Eves all at once! The smoke is clearing now. . . . Good God! The whole fountain is gone! And half of Henrik Ibsen, too! And everything is covered with . . . well, what actually is that? It looks like bubble bath suds."

"Do you think there are any survivors?"

The commandant lowered his field glasses and looked at the cannoneer. "Believe me, my dear cannoneer, even a Finn couldn't survive an explosion like that."

No and No and No

IT WAS ALL over.

Stanislaw stared blankly at the screens in front of him.

And they stared just as blankly back. Because everything was gone now: the *blop*, the *blip*, and the image of Nilly and the sleigh.

Stanislaw had spent several minutes yelling the name "Nilly" into the radio without receiving any answer.

And he hadn't heard anything from Victor or Lisa either.

The explosion, which could be heard throughout the entire city, must have gotten them all.

Stanislaw stood up and walked out to the hangar cave, where a cold wind was blowing in from outside. He walked all the way out to the end by the takeoff ramp, pushed aside a branch of the spruce tree, and stared down at the fjord below. It was starting to get light in the east, and he could hear fire truck and police car sirens, but no ambulances. Because you don't need ambulances when people are dead.

Stanislaw wiped away a tear.

Everything, absolutely *everything*, was lost. He wished he'd never said yes to saving Christmas. Or rather, he wished *he* was the one who'd been blown to smithereens down there in front of the National Theater Shopping Mall instead of Nilly, Lisa, Victor, and those poor reindeer. Stanislaw was 240 years old, so why should he—a man who didn't have anything to live for anymore—survive instead of good, nice people and animals who should have a long life ahead of them? Why should . . . ?

"Cuckoo!"

Stanislaw turned around. Did he hear that right? Had he just heard . . . ?

He hurried back to the Santa workshop.

And there sat Victor and Lisa, each flopped in a chair, huffing and panting. Both were covered with soap suds, and Victor held a charred cuckoo clock with a giraffe head under his arm.

"Y-y-you're alive!" Stanislaw cheered. "The explosion . . . How did you . . . ?"

"We managed to hide under Dolores," Doctor Proctor moaned.

"But Nilly and the reindeer, poor . . ."

Lisa started to cry.

"D-d-did you see them?" Stanislaw asked, and then put his hand over his mouth.

"The missile blew the whole fountain to bits," Doctor Proctor said, shaking his head. "We found pieces of the sleigh, fragments of the reins, et cetera."

"Terrible!" Stanislaw whispered. "And all these bubbles?"

"The time soap ended up in one of the jets of water in the fountain and, bam, bubbles everywhere."

"But . . ." Stanislaw took a deep breath. "If it bubbled up, then Nilly could conceivably have traveled back in time to another location?"

"That was the last glimmer of hope we had," Lisa sniffled. "But I told him to wish himself here to the

Santa workshop, and he should have been here by now." She covered her face with her hands. "And now he's gone forever!" she wailed. And then all three of them started crying.

They put their arms around one another and comforted one another as best they could, but it hurt so much that they just cried louder and louder.

"Shh!" Lisa said.

"Nooo!" Doctor Proctor sobbed. "I *need* to cry!"

"Me too!" Stanislaw bawled.

"Shh!" Lisa repeated, and moved away from the two blubbering grown-ups.

"Why?" Doctor Proctor sniffled.

"Listen!"

They stopped crying, and then they heard it, music. It was coming over the radio from the control panel.

Then the music stopped and they heard loud applause. Plus a familiar voice yelling, "Bravo, bravo! Encore, encore!"

"It's Nilly!" Lisa whispered.

"Møø!" the radio said.

"Those are my reindeer," Stanislaw whispered.

"Nilly!" Doctor Proctor said loudly. "This is head-quarters! Can you hear us?"

"Uh, yeah," said Nilly's voice. "Let's see. Yes, yeah, it seems like I can."

"Where are you?" Doctor Proctor asked.

"In Paris."

"Paris? What in the world are you doing in . . . ?"

"They're at the Moulin Rouge," Lisa said.

"Of course!" Doctor Proctor said, smacking his forehead.

"Huh?" Stanislaw said.

"They put on this cancan show there," Doctor Proctor explained. "You know, those dancers who stand on the stage and kick their legs way up in the air. Really long legs."

"Nilly *loves* cancan dancers," Lisa said. "Nilly, you were supposed to think about the Santa workshop!"

"I know," Nilly said. "But I didn't see any soap bubbles, so I thought it was all over. So I closed my eyes and thought about something nice. And I couldn't think of anything nicer than cancan dancing at the Moulin Rouge. I heard a splash, and when I opened my eyes again we were sitting here. . . . Hey, reindeer, what row are we sitting in?"

"Møø!"

"The fourth row! Not bad, right? The fourth row. We can see *everything*!"

"Come home," Lisa said.

"Yeah, yeah, soon. But right now we're calling for an encore and . . ."

"I'm not kidding, Nilly! Come home now!"

"So, uh, here's the thing. We don't have a sleigh anymore."

"Take the Paris flight to Oslo."

"I don't have any money, and I don't think they let reindeer on planes. No, I think we're probably going to have to stay here for a while. *Encore! Encore!*"

"Not to spoil your fun or anything, Nilly," Stanislaw said. "But I'm positive I can get some of my relatives in Paris to help set you up with a new sleigh."

"What kind of relatives?"

"Oh, I must have at least a dozen sons in Paris. Yes, daughters, too." Stanislaw realized that Doctor Proctor and Lisa were looking at him oddly. "Oh, come on! I'm *two hundred and forty* years old. A man's got to have a little fun in a quarter of a millennium. Maybe they don't all know I'm their father, but the ones who've lived to be more than a hundred and fifty probably realize they're not quite like other people. I could contact them on the Santa frequency and ask one of them to help Nilly."

"And tell them *what?*" Lisa asked. "'Hi, I'm your father. We haven't spoken since you were born a hundred years ago, but can you arrange a sleigh?'"

"Ingenious!" Stanislaw exclaimed, lighting up. "And here I've been brooding back and forth about how to phrase it. Thank you so much, little lady!" Stanislaw lunged across the desk and adjusted the radio frequency until the needle was pointing to SANTA FREQUENCY.

"Wait. Wait!" Lisa said. "You *can't* just say it like that!"

"I can't?"

"No, you have to . . . uh, give them a little time so they don't faint from shock."

"Hmm. You're right again, young lady."

Stanislaw cleared his throat, tugged on his beard for a

minute, then pushed a button and in a formal voice said:

"To all the dear Santas out there. Many of you will be afraid now because you're suddenly hearing a voice in your head, an unfamiliar voice at that. But hearing this voice just means that you have Santa blood in your veins. Which is to say that you're related to me, Santa Claus. Exactly how closely we're related is something we can come back to later. What's important now is that I need help finding a sleigh in Paris and . . ."

"And maybe you should say this in French, so your relatives in Paris will understand you," Lisa said.

"Yes, good point! Uh . . . *parlez-vous français?* Uhh . . . *Je suis Saint Nicolas* . . . Uhh . . . Nilly *est un garçon* in need of assistance . . . uhh . . ."

While Stanislaw bumbled his way along in French, Doctor Proctor and Lisa walked over to the fireplace to warm themselves up.

"Well, there goes Christmas," Doctor Proctor

said, eyeing the elf robots that were still making and wrapping presents, which were amassing in a massive pile at the end of the long gift-wrapping table. "Even if we do get Nilly home, we won't get all the Christmas presents delivered now, not since the rest of the time soap wound up in the fountain."

"I know," Lisa said, looking at the empty picture frame over the fireplace. "But at least in a way we did get *Nilly* a Christmas present."

"We did indeed."

"Isn't it strange?" Lisa said. "Every Christmas we just think about all the new stuff we're going to get. But we forget that an even bigger Christmas gift is being lucky enough to keep all the wonderful things we already have."

"Hmm."

"That's the only Christmas present I'm going to wish for from now on, to get to hold on to everyone I love, like Nilly, you and Juliette, my mom and dad. To get to keep the house we live in, my dad's old car, and my bed, because it's so good. And the Game Boy I inherited from my Uncle Torjus. And the princess shoes you and Juliette gave me for Christmas last year. I wouldn't trade any of those for . . . for . . . well, I can hardly think of anything I don't already have. We have everything. It's just too bad that Thrane Inc. cheated all the people who might have really needed a Christmas present out of it."

"You're a smart girl, Lisa," Doctor Proctor said with a smile.

"I know," Lisa said, squinting at the empty picture frame. "What does that say, right there?" She pointed.

"Say?" Doctor Proctor said. "It doesn't say anything. It's an empty frame."

"Look in the corner of the frame. It looks like a little piece of the picture tore off and is still in there."

The professor got up on his tiptoes and adjusted his swim goggles.

"Hmm, you're right. It's a small piece of torn paper, and it says Oslo District Court. Why?"

"Can you pick me up so I can look at it more closely?"

"All right. Although there's not really much to look at in an empty picture frame," Doctor Proctor said, and bent down so Lisa could climb up and sit on his shoulders. Then he stood back up.

"Not the empty one," Lisa said as she swayed back and forth on top of the skinny, wobbly genius inventor. "The other one. Two steps to your right, please. Yeah, like that."

Lisa studied the old photograph of all the elves gift wrapping under a younger Stanislaw's watchful eye. She leaned closer. And there in the picture, over the fireplace, hung the same empty frame. Only it wasn't empty. In the picture the frame contained something that looked like a letter. It looked like it was a written document, anyway.

"Hey, did you bring the mega-super-ultra-magnifying-glass?" Lisa asked.

"Always," Doctor Proctor said, and wobbled even more as he let go of one of Lisa's feet and pulled a magnifying glass out of his jacket pocket.

"Thanks," Lisa said, and took the magnifying glass, which actually looked remarkably normal. "How do I activate the mega-super-ultra-enlargement?" she asked.

"Push the button on the handle where it says mega-super-ultra . . ."

"I see it. Now, try to stand *totally* still." Lisa pushed the button, and immediately she was able to see the writing on the framed letter. In one corner, sure enough, it said Oslo District Court. And the title said DEED OF REGISTRATION. She proceeded to read out loud:

Oslo, 3rd July, 1822

All rights, appurtenances, privileges, and intellectual property associated with Christmas—including but not limited to Little Christmas Eve, Christmas Eve, Christmas Day proper, the Second Day of Christmas, the Third Day of Christmas, and all intervening holiday days between Christmas and New Year's—are hereby bargained, granted, sold, enfeoffed, set over, and confirmed as belonging unto Mr. Stanislaw Hansen, hereinafter called and known by the name of Santa Claus.

"Eureka!" Doctor Proctor exclaimed, but that set him wobbling and lurching so much from side to side that Lisa had to hold on tight to his thin wisps of hair to keep from falling off.

"Does that mean what I think it does?" Lisa said.

"Yes, it does!"

"Stanislaw!" Lisa adjusted herself upright a little, then dismounted, sliding down Doctor Proctor's back. She ran over to the former Santa Claus.

"*Merci, merci, Isabelle*," Stanislaw said into the microphone before turning to Lisa. "The sleigh is all taken care of," he said. "Nilly should be here in about forty-five minutes or so."

"The king didn't own Christmas," Lisa said. "You did!"

"Me?"

"Yes! It was registered in your name! Don't you remember?"

"I'm two hundred and forty years old, Lisa. So many things have happened. . . . But, you know, actually, now that you mention it, I think I do remember registering my ownership of Christmas sometime back in the eighteen hundreds."

"It was in 1822! You even had a document proving

it, a framed deed of registration that used to hang over the fireplace!"

"The deed of registration from over the fireplace!" Stanislaw exclaimed. "Of course, how could I forget?"

"That means," Doctor Proctor said, "that Mr. Thrane's agreement with the king is invalid, and that Thrane Inc. doesn't own Christmas. *Everyone* has the right to celebrate it!"

"Hurray!" Lisa cheered. "Christmas is back!"

"Um . . . ," Doctor Proctor began.

"What is it?" Lisa asked.

"Well, if Stanislaw doesn't remember what he did with the deed of registration . . ."

"Stanislaw?" Lisa said.

Stanislaw slumped lower and lower in his chair, looking at them with sad, puppy-dog eyes.

"You . . . you haven't forgotten . . . ?" Lisa began.

Stanislaw shrugged.

"You don't have any idea?" Doctor Proctor asked.

"Not the foggiest." Stanislaw sighed.

"All right. All right," Lisa said. "It's no big deal. Juliette told me that they keep a copy of all the deeds at the courthouse. Luckily."

"Phew. Luckily," Doctor Proctor said.

"Luckily!" Stanislaw cried, relieved. "Ho-ho, luckily!"

LUCKILY, MR. THRANE thought.

Luckily, he had managed to claw his way out of the frigid water, back up onto the ice, and crawl over to the islet with the lighthouse decorated with the pretty pine boughs. Luckily, it was only twenty-two degrees out and not, say, twelve degrees, since, unluckily, he was soaking wet. Luckily, he had a lighter, which still worked, and luckily, there was some driftwood under the snow to make a bonfire. But unluckily, he didn't have any kindling. If only he were lucky enough to have a piece of dry paper he could have used, the way he'd set fire to that dry, brittle deed of registration he'd found at the court-house in Oslo.

He'd gone there after he'd bought Christmas from the king, to register Thrane Inc. as the new owner of Christmas.

"First we have to check and make sure that no one already owns this Christmas you speak of," the old, gray-haired registrar had told him in her creaky voice, sitting there behind a dusty desk in a dusty office with dusty windows and flipping through a binder of registration deeds that were so dry and old that they looked like they would turn into dust soon themselves. And right when Mr. Thrane thought she would snap the binder shut and say that no one else owned Christmas, she had pointed a crooked finger at a very old piece of paper.

"What's this?" she had said. "Looks like a someone named . . ." She had pushed her thick glasses farther up her nose and leaned closer to the sheet of paper. ". . . Stanislaw Hansen already owns Christmas and has since 1822."

Mr. Thrane had coughed a single cough, and she had looked up at him. "Mold," he'd said. "It causes coughing."

"Oh, really?"

"On the wall behind you," Mr. Thrane said. "It's not so easy for the untrained eye to see, but I'm a fungal inspector, and that there is a massive mold infestation." Then he had coughed.

And the gullible elderly woman had turned around and studied the wall thoroughly for a long time, while Mr. Thrane had coughed so loudly that she couldn't hear the sound of a piece of paper being unceremoniously ripped out of a binder.

"I don't see anything," she had finally said.

"At your age, your eyesight probably isn't what it once was," Mr. Thrane had said commiseratively. "I thought, for example, that you said there was something about Christmas on the registration deed in front of you, but as far as I can see, it's about an Edna Sivertsen, who's registered a deed on a parcel of land for a vacation cabin in Hurum."

"That's funny," the registrar had said, staring at the sheet of paper in the binder. She had wrinkled her nose so her glasses came closer to her eyes. "But it looks like you're right. Yes, well, then, Mr. Thrane, in that case we can write you a deed of registration to show that Christmas is yours."

When Mr. Thrane had walked out onto the street outside the courthouse in Oslo that day, he had pulled the crumpled registration deed belonging to Stanislaw Hansen out of his pocket, set it on fire with his lighter, and used it to light up the long, fat cigar he had stuck between his big, wet lips. And then he'd laughed the most wicked laugh, absolutely the best—in terms of wickedness—laugh in the world.

He laughed very wickedly now as he thought back on it, too, because—even though he wasn't going to win this year's snowman contest and he was colder right now than any dog had ever been—he owned Christmas. Christmas was his, his and his alone, and no one could do anything about it. So *ho-ho-ho*! Luckily, it was almost morning. Then the Nesodden ferry would start shuttling commuters back and forth and it would be guaranteed to pick him up. Mr. Thrane saw something move across the sky, way up above the lighthouse. That must be the flight from Paris. At least it was coming from the direction of Paris. But his vision must have started to go as well, because for an instant he thought he'd seen a Santa sleigh. Ah, but he wasn't seeing things now, because there came the Nesodden ferry. It was breaking a channel through the ice, because it had seen him. Luckily!

The Day before
Christmas Eve,

also Known as Little Christmas Eve in Norway, Except by People Who Can't Afford Christmas Presents, Who Are Forced to Call It "Little Eve" or Something

IT WAS THE morning of Little Christmas Eve.

"This super-cute French girl came over to us while we were watching the cancan performance and said we should go with her," Nilly explained as he, Lisa, and Doctor Proctor walked up the court-house steps.

"How did she find you?" Lisa asked.

"A teeny-tiny little boy with six reindeer inside the Moulin Rouge? I don't know. . . ."

"But she was able to hook you up with a sleigh?"

"Yeah. She said she had no idea she could just hammer together a sleigh simple as that. Or that she was related to Santa Claus. She said a voice just popped into her head that told her that stuff. Before the reindeer and I took off from Paris, I thanked her and gave her a big and very wet kiss on the cheek."

"I'm sure she really appreciated that," Lisa said wryly.

"Right?" Nilly said contentedly.

"Here it is," Doctor Proctor said, and then knocked on the door that said DEED REGISTRATION OFFICE.

"Come in!" a voice called from inside.

They opened the door and walked into a small, dusty office with filing cabinets lining its walls and tall stacks of paper piled on top of the cabinets. Behind a desk covered with several stacks of paperwork, they spotted a gray-haired woman with big eyeglasses that magnified her eyes so much they looked like two fried eggs.

"We're the ones who called about that registration deed that said Stanislaw Hansen owns Christmas," Doctor Proctor.

"I'm so sorry," the registrar said. "I've looked through all my binders, and the only copy of a deed I have is this one from a few weeks ago, and it says that Mr. Thrane—and no one else—owns Christmas."

"My beautiful, young madam," Nilly said.

"What?" the registrar said.

"I'm down here," Nilly said, and waited until she spotted him. "Monsieur Thrane's registration is a sham."

"Well, there was indubitably something dubitable about him. He claimed we had mold in here, and we've had it confirmed by the fungal inspector from Gjøvik himself that we *don't*. But without proof, I'm afraid there's not much I can do."

Our three friends trudged out of Oslo District Court, out into the midday sun, where people— the ones who could afford it, that is—were running around finishing their last-minute Christmas shopping.

"Now what do we do?" Lisa asked. "Stanislaw doesn't remember what happened to the deed."

"Yes, what do we do now?" Doctor Proctor sighed.

"Only one thing to do," Nilly said.

The other two turned to him.

He held up a long chain. Swinging back and forth at the end of the chain was his grandfather's old pocket watch.

"*Voilà*, as we say in Paris," he said.

"And that is . . . ?" Doctor Proctor asked.

"The solution," Nilly said.

"A . . . uh, timepiece that runs slightly fast?" Lisa asked.

"Hypnosis," Nilly whispered.

STANISLAW WAS SITTING in the chair in front of the control panel and leaned way back. His eyes were fixed on the pocket watch, which was swinging back and forth in front of his nose. The Santa workshop was completely quiet now. Doctor Proctor and Lisa sat with their arms folded and skeptical expressions while Nilly stood on a stool in front of the former Santa.

"You will keep your eyes on the watch," Nilly whispered. "You will relax completely. You are letting yourself slip into Doctor Nilly's deep hypnosis, where everything that happened from your childhood until now will come back to you. I will count backward from ten, and when I get to zero you will be hypnotized. Ten, nine, eight . . ."

Stanislaw's eyes slid shut.

"See that? Oh yeah," Nilly said, congratulating himself and stuffing his watch back into his pocket. "It was totally easy. Okay, Stanislaw, we're going to skip over your whole childhood and when you were a young man and all that and go straight to the registration deed that disappeared from the picture frame. What happened? Was it stolen? Why was it taken out of the frame? And where is it now?"

Nilly watched Stanislaw tensely. But he didn't make a sound.

"Stanislaw? Answer Doctor Nilly, please." Still not a peep.

"Stanislaw, where is the deed? We don't have all day here. Tomorrow is Christmas Eve."

Stanislaw's eyelids started twitching, and sounds emerged from his half-open mouth. Nilly leaned in closer. He tried to interpret the words, but they were incomprehensible. It sounded more like a large-toothed saw being slowly pulled over a piece of wood. Nilly looked at the flapping lips.

Stanislaw wasn't talking. He was snoring.

"Hey, that was hypnosis, not a lullaby! Hello in there? Wake up!" Nilly patted Stanislaw's cheek, but the snoring just got louder.

"He's had a few strenuous days, poor guy," Doctor Proctor said. "I mean, he's not a kid anymore."

"Now what do we do?" Lisa asked.

Just then one of the elf robots started bleating: "OUT OF PAPER! OUT OF PAPER!"

"Arg!" Lisa yelled, pressing her hands over her ears. "I forgot I was supposed to bring wrapping paper."

"And I remember . . ."

Lisa, Nilly, and Doctor Proctor turned toward Stanislaw, who was sitting up in his chair with his eyes wide.

"We were out of paper," Stanislaw said. "It was just

last year. The thought occurred to me that I ought to at least give one present to someone anyway. Santas get this urge as Christmas approaches. So I looked around for something I could use to wrap my present in, something I didn't need. And my eyes came to rest on that piece of paper in the frame."

". . . which was the proof that you own Christmas," Lisa pointed out.

"Yes, and since I had stopped being Santa, it was a piece of paper I didn't need anymore. Honestly, it was just an irritating reminder of what was lost. So I took it out and . . ."

". . . used it as wrapping paper?" Nilly asked in disbelief.

"Yup," Stanislaw said, and then yawned.

"That's that, then," Nilly said. "Our proof that the king and Mr. Thrane never owned Christmas is in a landfill or incinerated."

"I don't suppose you remember who you gave the

present to or the address where the person lives?" Lisa asked.

"I don't, no," Stanislaw said. The others sighed.

"But I remember where," Stanislaw said.

"What do you mean where?" Lisa asked. "You just said you don't remember the address. . . ."

"Fifty-nine degrees, fifty-four minutes, and forty seconds north," Stanislaw said. "And ten degrees, forty-four minutes, and two-point-three seconds east." Lisa and Nilly just stared at him.

"Santas," Doctor Proctor said after clearing his throat, "never forget the coordinates of a place they've delivered a present to. It's stored in their memories forever. Now we just need to figure out exactly what place those coordinates correspond to. Let's see . . ."

Doctor Proctor leaned over the control panel and pushed some buttons to enlarge the map on the screen.

"Why did you deliver the present to that specific place?" Nilly asked.

"Good question. I can't remember. I probably checked the nice-child-ometer and found the kid there."

"You did!" Doctor Proctor said. "And you couldn't be bothered to go very far either. You were right here in Oslo . . . at number fourteen Cannon Avenue!"

"Fourteen?" Lisa exclaimed.

"Of course!" Nilly said. "The nicest girl! Obviously, that's you, Lisa."

"The snow globe? That was from you?"

"Looks like it," Stanislaw said.

"But then the deed may not have been incinerated or thrown away," Nilly said. "I mean, your mom saves all the wrapping paper, right? She even irons it. Yippee! We can present freshly ironed proof that the king and Mr. Thrane never owned Christmas."

"Let's go!"

TWO MINUTES AND sixteen seconds later Nilly and the jet reindeer surreptitiously landed behind the garage in Doctor Proctor's yard.

"I'll be right back," Lisa said. She hopped out and ran toward the gate onto Cannon Avenue.

"Oh, good, there you are!" the commandant said, looking up from the table, which was set for breakfast, as she came storming into the kitchen. "I was just about to go upstairs and wake you up. Strange, though. . . . It sounded like you came in from outside."

"Good morning," Lisa said as she opened one of the kitchen cupboards and started looking through the stash of gift wrap of all colors and patterns. "Are you going to work?"

"No. We earned a little time off, because while you were safely asleep in your warm bed, your father has been up all night defending the country. We just shot down a Finnish jet fighter." The commandant took a loud, self-satisfied gulp from his coffee cup. "What do you say to that, my dear?"

"I hope no one was injured," Lisa said with a concentrated, concerned expression as she continued flipping through the wrapping paper.

"You hope no one—injuring someone is sort of the *point* when you shoot a missile, my dear. And the Finn was probably quite injured. There wasn't a scrap of him or his plane left." The commandant set down his cup. "Unfortunately, the fountain sustained some damage as well. Yes, to tell you the truth, both the Henrik Ibsen statue and the National Theater Shopping Mall have seen better days." The commandant looked out the window. "I really hope we don't have to shoot any more missiles. Oslo needs its public squares. And I'm sure Finland needs its Finns as well."

"I can't find it!" Lisa wailed, on the verge of tears.

"Can't find what, sweetie?" asked her mother, who had just walked into the kitchen.

"That weird wrapping paper that was around the snow globe I got for Christmas last year. The one that said 'from Santa' on it."

"Oh, that one," her mother said, and sat down at the table and started buttering a slice of bread. "You don't need to look for that one, sweetie."

"Oh?"

"I used it to wrap that present you asked me to give Nilly's mother the other day."

"What? But that present was already wrapped!"

"Yes, but it was wrapped in such an awfully fancy, expensive-looking paper, I thought, considering the present was just for Nilly."

"*Just* for Nilly? Mom, he's my best friend!"

"Yes, and your father and I are a little concerned about that . . . that you don't have other friends. I mean, honestly, he is a little . . ."

"A little what?"

"Well, a little . . . uh . . . what should we say?"

"Unusual," the commandant said, and finished the rest of his coffee.

"Why not use the lovely wrapping paper that was on Nilly's present and give a Christmas present to someone who could become your friend, someone a little more . . . uh . . ."

"Un-unusual," the commandant said.

Lisa slammed the cupboard door shut, then the kitchen door, and then finally the front door.

"Where is she going?" her mother asked.

"To school, I assume," the commandant said, and yawned.

"It's Little Christmas Eve. They're off today," her mother said, and took a bite of her buttered bread, now with a slice of Jarlsberg cheese on top.

"Which reminds me that we have a thorough housecleaning ahead of us, so quit your yawning."

"Thorough housecleaning," the commandant moaned, and then closed his eyes and wondered which was less appealing: mopping the floors or having the Finns attack again so he had an excuse to go back to work.

"THE PAPER WENT to your mom," an out-of-breath Lisa yelled as she returned to the sleigh.

"Oy," Nilly said. "Come on."

They ran out onto Cannon Avenue and had just walked through the front gate at the yellow house when they heard a powerful detonation from inside. It shook the windows and rattled snow off the roof.

"Yikes. What was that?" Lisa asked.

"I have a hunch," Nilly said, running up the front steps and opening the door. "Mom? Mom!"

"Yes!" a jubilant voice replied. "Yes!"

Nilly ran to the bathroom door. "Is everything *going* okay in there, Mom?"

"It's never *gone* better, Nilly my boy!"

"How's your . . . backlog?"

"The logjam finally broke—just now! Ahhhhh. I've never felt lighter! What do you want for Christmas, dear?"

"Good parents," Nilly muttered under his breath, and then pulled Lisa into the living room.

"That's a strikingly green Christmas tree you've

got there," Lisa said, and watched while Nilly rifled through the presents under the tree.

"Yeah, they tend to be green when they're made of plastic," Nilly said, and then started reading the tags out loud: "'From Tim to Krystal, my gorgeous plaything.' 'From Roy to Krystal, here's hoping it's one hell of a Christmas.' 'From Stein-Ove to Krystal, a little something to wear when we meet again.' 'From Kurt to Krystal, my . . . ' Blah, blah, blah. Lisa, I don't see any presents here from you."

"And I don't see the wrapping paper either," Lisa said. "But my mom said she gave the present to your mom."

"Okay," Nilly said. "But why didn't you do it yourself?"

"Honestly, because I'm a little scared of your mom."

"Oh, she just gets a little grumpy when she's constipated," Nilly said. "Come on."

They walked back to the bathroom door.

"Mom?"

"Yes, dear?"

"Where's the present Lisa's mother brought over?"
Silence from the bathroom.

"Mom!"

"Yes, yes, yes, I took it. All right?"

"She took it?" Lisa whispered in disbelief.

Nilly shrugged and yelled, "Where is it now,
Mom?"

"How should I know?"

"You must have some idea."

"Nope. I unwrapped it, and that little girl must
have a chunk of change, because it was a new mouthpiece for your trumpet. That made it way easier for
me to sell the trumpet."

"You *sold* the trumpet?"

"I advertised it online. Man, I got four thousand
crowns for it! With what I borrowed from Roy, I
think I've got enough to celebrate Christmas now. And

now that I'm free of all that stress, my clogged pipes have finally cleared too! Aren't you happy for me?"

"The wrapping paper, Mom. Where's the wrapping paper?"

"Huh? I'm holding that in my hand right here. I was just about to . . ."

"Mom, no!"

"Huh? Isn't an until-recently-constipated woman allowed to wipe?"

"Not with that!" Nilly yelled frantically, jumping up and down. "Does it say anything on it?"

"Say, schmay . . . It's a little hard to tell since it already has a couple of . . . uh, skid marks on it. But, yeah, I guess it does say something: D-E-E-D-O-F-R-E-G-I-S-T-R-A-T-I-O-N and something about someone named Stanislaw owning Christmas. Geez. But right now I need it to—"

"Mom! Let go of that paper! Now!"

Eight Hours until Christmas Eve.

Although, Since They Weren't Able to Save Christmas, People Will Have to Forget About It and Look Forward to Other Holidays Instead, Like That Day in July That Commemorates Saint Olof's Death at the Battle of Stiklestad in AD 1030 or Whitmonday

IT WAS FOUR o'clock in the afternoon on Little Christmas Eve, December 23rd, and already many people had gathered in front of the National Theater Shopping Mall. They were waiting for the king's extremely official and very ceremonial ribbon cutting to kick off the last-minute Christmas shopping. The stores had closed for one hour in the middle of the day to do inventory and figure out what they still had too much of so they could lower the prices on those items and, hopefully, sell them before the Christmas sales period ended and people started thinking about things besides buying stuff. And after the king kicked off the last-minute Christmas shopping in a moment, the stores were going stay open *all* night until two p.m. tomorrow, Christmas Eve. An expectant murmur ran through the crowd as a black king limousine pulled up to the curb in front of the red carpet that led to the National Theater Shopping Mall. A policeman with a Fu Manchu mustache opened the rear passenger door, and out stepped the king and his court marshal.

"Good gracious, what happened here?" the king asked. "What happened to the fountain? And the Ibsen sculpture?"

"They blew up last night, Your Majesty," the policeman said. A fat man jogged down the red carpet toward them.

"Good morning, Your—*ah-ah-achoo*—Majesty!" Mr. Thrane proclaimed. "Sorry I'm late. I just came—*sniffle*—ashore."

The king cocked his head to the side and then asked, "You don't happen to own a fake nose with a mustache, do you, Mr. Thrane?"

"What?"

"And a boiler suit that says 'fungal inspector' on the back?"

"I'd be happy to wear anything so long as it was dry. That would be wonderful, but no."

"Hmm, you do look damp, actually, especially your hair."

"Took a little swim in the fjord this morning, and we're sold out of hair dryers."

"And your suspenders only have one strap, Mr. Thrane."

"The other one snapped when the missile made a sharp turn."

"When the . . . ?"

"My suspenders got snagged on a missile-that-never-misses, and I was pulled all over town before we went flying out over the fjord and . . ."

"Boooring." The king yawned. "Let's get this whole show on the road, so I can go home."

"Of course, of course!" Mr. Thrane put his arm around the king and escorted him down the red carpet. "Busy these days, Your Majesty?"

"Yes. I'm halfway through the third mission in Battlefield Finland, and Finland is winning."

"I understand. I understand. I just want you to say a few words about what a fine holiday Christmas is and mention our special deal on snowblowers. Then you'll thank me personally and cut the red ribbon across the entrance to the mall there."

"Are you sure I have reason to thank you, Mr. Thrane? A Doctor Proctor came to visit me and told me there isn't any mold in my basement."

"Doctor—*achoo*—Proctor? He's a mold infestation himself, so he's just saying that to protect other mold infestations."

"Really? I suppose he did look a bit moldish. But the children . . ."

"The children, yes. A busybody girl in pigtails and an unruly little lad with red hair? Juvenile delinquents, Your Majesty, rabble-rousers and fibbers of the worst sort. I wouldn't even dare let my twins near them."

"Are you saying I've been tricked again?"

"Turn around—*double achoo*—Your Majesty!"

They went to stand behind the red ribbon as people crowded closer so they could dash inside as soon as the department store opened. The king grabbed for the giant scissors lying on a nearby table, but Mr. Thrane was quicker and snatched them for himself.

"A few nice words about me and snowblowers first," he whispered. "*Then* you cut the ribbon."

The king mumbled his annoyance. Then he cleared his throat.

"My dear fellow countrymen, countrywomen, and subjects," he said. "It is in wishing you a merry Christmas, even better snowblowers, and no mold that I hereby . . ." He reached for the scissors, but Mr. Thrane would not let go of them.

"Thank me," Mr. Thrane hissed.

". . . and so I would like to thank Mr. Thrane, the owner of this store. And with that I hereby declare the last-minute Christmas shopping season—"

"Remind the idiots that they need to spend at least ten thousand crowns," Thrane hissed, beaming at the crowd.

"Good point," the king said. "Remember: You'll need to turn your pockets inside out and buy, buy, buy if you want to celebrate Christmas. You actually need to purchase ten thousand—"

"No!" a little, busybody girl's voice called out from the crowd.

"No?" the king said, surprised.

"No!" an even smaller, unruly boy's voice replied.

"No?" the court marshal asked, sternly eyeing the crowd.

"No!" a doctor's voice repeated.

"No?" Mr. Thrane scoffed.

"No!" thundered a Santa Claus voice.

And with that four people we know well stepped up to the red ribbon.

"Juvenile delinquents!" Mr. Thrane yelled and pointed. "Arrest them!"

"We just want to give you something," Lisa said, and held out a sheet of paper.

"Police!" Mr. Thrane bellowed.

"Coming!" they heard from the far side of the square. "Just as quickly as we can!"

"Stop right there!" the king said. "What *is* this?"

"It's a registration deed from 1822," Doctor Proctor said. "The contents of which should interest you."

"Plus some slight, minor skid marks, which . . . uh, shouldn't interest you," Nilly said.

The king put on his monocle and began reading.

"Why is he only wearing half a pair of eyeglasses?" someone in the crowd whispered.

"Maybe he's only farsighted in the one eye?" someone else replied.

"Maybe he couldn't afford a full set?" a third person suggested.

"Shh!" the king said. "I'm trying to read!"

"Shh!" the court marshal yelled. "His Royal Highness is reading!"

A silence settled over the square, yes, almost a

Christmas peace, and wouldn't you know, it started snowing just then too. Small snowflakes that wafted down and settled on the king's hair as he silently moved his lips, spelling his way through, line by line.

Then he removed his monocle, which is to say his single-lensed eyeglasses, snatched the scissors from Mr. Thrane, and looked out at the crowd.

"When I cut the ribbon with these scissors, you can go buy as *many* Christmas presents as you want," he said.

Mr. Thrane grinned even more broadly and gave his bulging belly a contented pat.

"Or you can buy as *few* as you want," the king said. "Or nothing at all. You will all get to celebrate Christmas anyway, because this document proves that Christmas never belonged to me. Rather, it belongs to a person named Stanislaw Hansen. And that means that Mr. Thrane has no say over who's allowed to celebrate Christmas or not."

"What?" Mr. Thrane spluttered. "I—I—*achoo*—protest!"

"Mr. Thrane," the king said. "Or perhaps we should say Mr. Fungal Inspector Enarht. You are hereby revealed!"

Then—with a little snip of the scissors—he cut through Mr. Thrane's remaining suspender strap. And it happened so quickly that Mr. Thrane didn't have time to grab his pants before they fell down around his white ankles and the entire crowd saw his unusually large underpants covered with little multi-colored cars—Hummers, of course.

"Merry Christmas!" the king proclaimed, handing the deed back to Lisa and walking back down the red carpet.

The crowd seemed to be holding its breath, yes, as if they hadn't quite understood or didn't quite believe what had just transpired.

Lisa saw two familiar figures pushing their way through the assemblage: an adult woman with a determined expression, her glasses down on the tip of her nose, and a girl with a bandage stuck to one eyeglass lens.

"Is it true, Lisa?" Mrs. Strobe panted once they reached the front of the crowd.

"Can we really celebrate Christmas, all of us?" Birte squeaked, her voice trembling.

"Yes!" Lisa said, smiling and waving Stanislaw's deed.

Mrs. Strobe turned to the crowd and announced, in her most attention-grabbing teacher's voice, which is to say her teacher's outdoor voice: "Lisa here says it's true! Christmas is ours, everyone!"

And the crowd burst into cheers. People hugged strangers, all exclaiming "Merry Christmas!" at the same time. Some even began to dance.

"Arrest the fat guy," the king told one of the two mustachioed policemen who were holding open the rear passenger door of his limousine.

"Of course, Your Royal Highness. What should we arrest him for?"

"Fraud, con artistry, reckless flying, off-season swimming, and public nudity. Take your pick."

And with that the king climbed into his limousine and returned to the palace.

And Now It Is Right
Before...

IT HAD GROWN dark in Oslo on the final night before the big day: Christmas Eve.

High in the hills above the city, by Lake Maridal, a farmer walked up the ramp to his barn to set out a bowl of Christmas porridge for the barn gnomes. It wasn't that he believed in barn gnomes—many people claimed they were purely mythological—but you could never be completely sure, could you? If they did happen to be real, you certainly didn't want to be on their bad side. And, indeed, most years when he came back to the barn on Christmas Eve, someone had pretty much always been in there and eaten up the porridge. On his way back from the barn, the farmer stopped and looked out at Lake Maridal, where a fox hurried across the frozen lake in the moonlight. And down the hill from him, down by the fjord, Oslo lay glittering like a jewel in the night. Then he went back inside for an evening by the hearth, where his wife and kids were waiting for him to join them in a game of Monopoly.

Down in Oslo there weren't so many people in the stores anymore. By now most people knew they didn't need to burn through all their savings in order to celebrate Christmas, so they'd gone home instead to finish their final preparations. They were decorating Christmas trees, hanging Christmas stars in the windows, and setting out sheaves of grain for the songbirds.

Soon Lisa, Nilly, and Doctor Proctor would be doing that as well. But right now they were sitting in the Santa workshop drinking no-skin hot chocolate—it wouldn't form a skin on top or get clumps. Victor Proctor's father, Doctor Hector, had invented it.

"I almost feel a little sorry for Mr. Thrane, actually," Lisa said. "Imagine having to go to jail on Little Christmas Eve."

"Kind of depends on how excited you are about spending Christmas with your family," Nilly said, and then loudly slurped his cocoa.

"Hmm," Doctor Proctor said, contemplating Nilly thoughtfully.

"Yes, yes," Stanislaw said, and got up from the control panel and pushed his way through the six-foot-deep sea of wrapped presents that now covered the entire workshop. "Good thing we got more wrapping paper."

He patted one of the elf robots on the head, and it blinked contentedly back at him and proceeded to wrap more presents.

"It's just too bad we don't have any more time soap," Lisa said. "Without that we're not going to be able to deliver the presents to all the children who had maybe hoped to get something tomorrow."

"Right?" Nilly said.

"So, why are you still making presents, Stanislaw?"

Stanislaw poured hot chocolate into his cup. "Hmm, good question."

They watched him while he took a looong drink then wiped his mouth. "Did you guys hear that?" he asked.

"Hear what?"

"Shh!"

They listened. And there, they heard it: a møø!

Yes, it was an authentic reindeer møø! But it didn't come from the stall in the workshop where the jet reindeer were lying down chewing their cud. The sliding door that led out to the hangar cave creaked and then slid open. Cold air blew in and a round, red-cheeked face came into view in the doorway. It was a young man.

"*Guten Abend.*" He smiled. "Ich bin Günther."

"Good evening, Günther." Stanislaw smiled back. He walked over to Günther and flung out his arms. "I'm so glad to finally meet you."

The two gave each other a heartfelt hug that lasted for a long time.

"They kind of look alike, don't they?" Lisa whispered. "A little, anyway?"

"They look a lot alike," Doctor Proctor said.

Stanislaw and Günther stood off by themselves for a bit, speaking German with each other. Then Stanislaw turned to our three friends.

"Günther works as a letter carrier. He says he just about ran his bicycle off the road when a voice in his head claimed to be Santa Claus."

Günther laughed and said something quickly in German with a bunch of rolled *R*s and plenty of dative and accusative. Stanislaw chuckled and nodded.

"Günther said that at first he was shocked when this Santa Claus said he was summoning all his children into service," Stanislaw explained. "But he felt a strange joy and eagerness when the voice said that in two hours a sleigh pulled by young jet reindeer would land right outside all their homes and fly them to Oslo as quick as a flash."

"And Günther believed that?" Doctor Proctor asked. "He didn't think he was just losing his mind?"

"He's a Santa," Stanislaw said, patting Günther on the shoulder. "He didn't know it until now, but deep down inside he's been waiting for this his whole life. When it finally happens, he'll understand everything.

He gets that he's going to be Santa tonight and fly around with presents. Isn't that so, Günther?"

Günther nodded, smiling.

"But just Günther isn't going to be enough," Lisa said. Stanislaw translated this for Günther, and they both laughed.

"*Komm hier!*" Günther said, and waved for our friends to follow him. And they all walked out the door to the hangar cave in a collective herd.

"Yowza!" Nilly blurted out.

Because before them sat not one, but four, five, yes, six sleighs, all with teams of jet reindeer, and seated in five of the sleighs was a person who looked slightly confused but also very happy. Stanislaw walked around and embraced each one and talked a little with them.

"This is Miguel," Stanislaw called out. "He's a furniture mover in Salvador, Brazil, and he says he dropped the piano on his coworker's foot when he heard the voice in his head. He'll be delivering the Christmas presents throughout the state of Bahia in northeastern Brazil! And this is my daughter Betty. She was dressed as an elf in a toy store in Los Angeles when she heard my voice. She'll be handling Santa Monica, Hollywood, and the rest of LA County. She actually has time to come in for some hot chocolate, since most of the families in her territory won't open their presents until Christmas morning. Betty, I'm so happy to finally meet you."

The siblings greeted each other, conversed excitedly, and then gave one another a hug. And even though Stanislaw was laughing, tears were rolling down his cheeks.

"Cool sleighs!" Nilly said, and walked over to inspect one of them. "I didn't know they came in silver, too! But how much weight can these jet reindeer handle?"

"They're young. They can't handle all the weight

in the world. That's why we have multiple sleighs," Stanislaw said.

"But even six Santas isn't that many," Doctor Proctor said. "Not when you have to fly everywhere in the world with—"

"Look!" Lisa interrupted him. "Look!" Our friends turned around.

Lisa had pushed aside the branches on the big fir tree. "Well, I never!" Doctor Proctor exclaimed in a hushed tone.

"Cool," Nilly whispered. "Or actually, double cool."

They were staring out over the fjord, enchanted. The sun was just setting on the horizon and coloring the sky orange and red. And way out there they saw dots approaching, dots that grew and became sleighs with miniature jet reindeer pulling them. There were a lot of them. And there were even more behind them. There were sleighs as far as the eye could see.

"A whole armada of Santas is coming," Lisa whispered, spellbound.

Nilly took a breath and said, "Okay, maybe triple cool."

"It's going to be crowded in here," Stanislaw said. "We'd better start loading gifts onto the sleighs that are already here and getting them on their way so you can go home to your families."

"Couldn't I stay here and help out?" Nilly asked. "Please?"

"Sorry, Nilly, this is Santa work. We were born to do this, so we do it faster without help, you understand? Don't you have things to do at home?"

Nilly hung his head. "Apart from getting yelled at, I don't know what that would be."

"Well," Doctor Proctor said, and winked at Lisa, "I can think of one thing anyway. Come on, now. I think Juliette is waiting for us."

And as new sleighs landed on the takeoff and

landing ramp, our three friends said good-bye to Stanislaw.

They walked through the Santa workshop to the door that led to the train tunnel. Nilly walked slower than the other two, running his hand along the table, the fireplace, and the robots as if he knew this were the last time he would see them.

"Are you coming?" Doctor Proctor asked from the doorway.

"Soon," Nilly said, and ran over to the stall where his reindeer were and hugged them.

"Møø-rry Christmas," he said.

"Møø," they replied.

Nilly poured another cup of hot chocolate.

"Haven't you had enough hot chocolate yet?" Lisa asked.

"Oh, it's not for me," Nilly said, and took the cup with him.

They strolled through the train tunnel. A red glow shone in the darkness ahead of them.

"Hi, Tommy," Nilly said as they reached the glow. "Maybe this would taste good with your cigar?" He handed the cup of hot chocolate to the man, who stared at them with wide, terrified eyes.

"Nothing to be scared of," Nilly said. "I promise, there's *no* skin on top and *no* clumps of cocoa powder."

"It's not the skin or the clumps. I just wonder why you're being so nice," Tommy said. "It makes me r-r-really nervous."

"Because I'm pretty sure that if you found me sitting in a train tunnel someday you would bring me hot chocolate," Nilly said.

"And if you want to celebrate Christmas with us on Cannon Avenue, you're invited, Tommy," Doctor Proctor said.

"Thanks for the invitation, but I prefer to be alone. And I have everything I want here." Tommy grinned, took a drag from his cigar, and raised his hot chocolate.

"Apart from a Christmas ham," Nilly said.

"Well," Tommy said, "a miracle like that this year is more than a man can hope for."

"Maybe so, maybe so," Doctor Proctor said, and winked knowingly to Lisa and Nilly. "Good-bye, Tommy."

When our three friends emerged from the tunnel, they slowly strolled through the streets of the city and nodded, said hello, and wished people they didn't know a merry Christmas.

Out in front of city hall they managed to catch the streetcar that ran over toward Cannon Avenue.

"Everyone is so happy," Lisa said, smiling back at an elderly woman she'd given her seat to.

"That's what a proper Christmas does to people,"

Doctor Proctor said. "What are you thinking about, Nilly?"

Nilly had his button nose pressed against the streetcar window. He was staring longingly up at the sky.

"Flying a sleigh," he said. "It's one of the most amazing things I've done in my whole life."

"Good. It's important to appreciate all the fun things we *have* done, not just the fun things we're *going* to do," Doctor Proctor said.

"But what if all the fun is behind us now and there's no more ahead of us?" Nilly asked.

"Pshaw," Doctor Proctor said. "Nothing is more fun than a new adventure, right?"

"Riiiiight . . . ," Nilly and Lisa both said in unison.

"And there are always new adventures ahead of us. That's why they're called *new*. Get it?"

Lisa nodded. Nilly thought it over and then nodded as well.

They got off the streetcar into the snowy weather and walked up Cannon Avenue. All the windows were lit up, but none were as warm and cozy as the lights in the windows of the crooked, slightly peculiar blue house that sat all the way at the end of the street. They stomped their feet and brushed the snow off themselves on the front steps, left their shoes in the entryway, and walked into the kitchen, where Juliette was stirring a pot of rice porridge.

"I'm so excited to see you guys," she said. "Tell me *everything* that happened."

And so they did while they gobbled up porridge and laughed and Nilly used his arms and legs to act out some of the things that had happened.

When they were done, Juliette clapped her hands.

"*Mon Dieu*, it sounds like you've saved Christmas for everyone!"

"My modesty requires me to say that you're exaggerating," Nilly said, and then licked the last bits of rice porridge off his spoon. "But my honesty commands me to tell the truth: You are quite right. Nilly, Lisa, and Doctor Proctor saved Christmas for the western and eastern hemispheres. Or to be even more succinct than necessary: for the whole world."

Lisa laughed. Just then the cuckoo clock that Doctor Proctor must have nailed up on the wall sometime earlier in the day started to rumble.

"Oh no!" Lisa gasped and ducked.

The shutters popped open and a vampire giraffe head came out. But this time it reached only barely out of the opening, where it couldn't do any harm, and snapped its mouth "cuckoo" ten times before disappearing back into the clock again.

"I'm afraid the neck was lost in the explosion," Doctor Proctor said. "But anyway, now it's bedtime."

"Yeah." Lisa yawned.

"Already?" Nilly sighed. "Did we really remember to do everything we usually do on Little Christmas Eve?"

"Eat rice porridge, tell the stories of all the things we've done together since we became friends, put some food out for the songbirds, put the star on top of the Christmas tree, and danced the Proctor dance. Yup, I think that's pretty much it," Juliette said. "I guess the only thing left is that you haven't played 'Silent Night' on the trumpet yet."

"Oh, right. Yeah." Nilly sighed. "I don't have that trumpet anymore, so I can never play 'Silent Night' again."

"Remember: New adventures await us," Doctor Proctor said.

"Yes, that's why they're called new," Lisa said.

And with that the friends went their separate ways.

When Nilly walked in the door of the yellow house, he yelled, "Hi. I'm home!" and went straight to his room.

He lay down on his bed and stared at the ceiling. His door opened.

"Nilly?"

"Yes, Mom?" He sighed.

She sat down on the edge of his bed. "Hey you. I've been doing some thinking. Well, not just some but quite a bit of thinking. And I've decided I need to ask you for a little pre-Christmas gift."

"No, Mom, you can't have the pocket watch or the *Animals You Wish Didn't Exist* book!"

"That's not what I was going to ask you for, my boy. I need to ask for something bigger."

"Bigger?"

"Yes, I need to ask you to forgive me for being so grumpy and self-centered. The constipation . . . well, you know. And while you think about whether or not you're going to forgive me, here's an early Christmas present to you from me. And Lisa."

Nilly's mother held up a small black suitcase that looked brand-new. Nilly took it in astonishment and opened it.

"My trumpet!" he yelled. "With a new mouth-piece!"

"I found the guy I sold it to," his mother said, "and explained to him how foolish I'd been. So he let me buy it back. Plus, I bought a case so you don't have to keep it hanging on the wall."

"Thank you! Thank you so much, Mom!" He took out the trumpet.

She stood up and said, "Good night."

"Mom?"

"Yes?"

"Come here."

He sat up and then stood up on the bed and gave her a good, long hug, the kind you might usually save until Christmas.

"Does that mean I'm forgiven?" his mom asked with tears in her eyes.

"Of course," he said. "I know it's not always easy being my mother."

"Good thing you're not big on holding grudges," she said.

"Or, as some might say, I'm not big, period," he joked.

She laughed and wiped away her tears. "We'll have a lovely Christmas, Nilly. Just wait and see."

After his mother left his room, Nilly walked over to the window, opened it, and put his trumpet to his lips. Then, as the snow gently covered Cannon

Avenue with a beautiful crystalline carpet, he played "Silent Night" so peacefully and quietly that he knew he wouldn't wake anyone. Only those who really wanted to hear would hear. And when he was finished, he put his trumpet back into its beautiful new case, got undressed, put on his pajamas, and went to bed.

Then he closed his eyes, smiled happily, and immediately started dreaming of new adventures.

And they all lived happily ever—no, wait! There actually seems to be one very short chapter left.

It's After Midnight,

so It's December Twenty-Fourth and Christmas Eve Has Only Just Barely Begun

A NOISE WOKE Nilly up. He stared at his ceiling. It had been the sound of an animal. He was completely sure of that. He stared at the spine of *Animals You Wish Didn't Exist*. But no, something told him that this had been the sound of an animal you actually wished *did* exist. And then there was a distant scratchy sound: "Headquarters to Nilly!"

Nilly leaped out of bed, ran over to the window, and pulled the curtain aside.

And there, bobbing in midair in the moonlight, was a silver sleigh heaped full of gift-wrapped presents. There were six juvenile jet reindeer harnessed to it, treading air impatiently.

"Møø," they said.

"Headquarters to Nilly." The sound was coming from the earpiece sitting atop of the mound of presents. Nilly grabbed it and pushed it into his ear.

"Nilly here!"

"Hi, Nilly." It was Stanislaw's voice. "It looks like we're one Santa short. We need someone to deliver presents in southern Portugal. Do you think you can help us?"

"Yiiippyyy!"

And *there*! That's where this Christmas story ends,

as a little red-haired boy lowers the reins, whispers "møø," and there's a *whoosh* through the air. And people who look up into the sky see a glowing streak traveling over the city from somewhere above Cannon Avenue. Those of them who haven't read this book might think it's a shooting star, a comet, a satellite, or the flight from Paris. Something boooring. But you and I, we know what it is. We look at each other and wink, but we don't say anything. Because no one would believe us anyway.